T0115681

PHILIP K. DICK'S ELECTRIC DREAMS

BOOKS BY PHILIP K. DICK

The Exegesis of Philip K. Dick
Selected Stories of Philip K. Dick

NOVELS

The Broken Bubble
Clans of the Alphane Moon
Confessions of a Crap Artist
The Cosmic Puppets
Counter-Clock World
The Crack in Space
Deus Irae (with Roger Zelazny)
The Divine Invasion
Do Androids Dream of Electric Sheep?
Dr. Bloodmoney
Dr. Futurity
Eye in the Sky
Flow, My Tears, the Policeman Said
Galactic Pot-Healer
The Game-Players of Titan
Gather Yourselves Together
Lies, Inc.
The Man in the High Castle
The Man Who Japed
Martian Time-Slip
Mary and the Giant
A Maze of Death
Nick and the Glimmung
Now Wait for Last Year
Our Friends from Frolix 8
The Penultimate Truth
A Scanner Darkly
The Simulacra
Solar Lottery
The Three Stigmata of Palmer Eldritch
Time Out of Joint
The Transmigration of Timothy Archer
Ubik
Ubik: The Screenplay
VALIS
Vulcan's Hammer
We Can Build You
The World Jones Made
The Zap Gun

PHILIP K. DICK

✢

PHILIP K. DICK'S
ELECTRIC DREAMS

✢

HOUGHTON MIFFLIN HARCOURT
Boston   New York

CONTENTS

Introduction by Ronald D. Moore

Story title: Exhibit Piece
Script Title: Real Life

Ronald D. Moore is an American screenwriter and producer. He is best known for developing the re-imagined Battlestar Galactica series, for which he won a Hugo and a Peabody Award, and for Outlander, based on the novels of Diana Gabaldon. He began his career as a writer/producer on Star Trek: The Next Generation and Star Trek: Deep Space Nine.

The first time I read this piece it was in the context of looking for a PKD story to adapt for *Electric Dreams*. Right from the start, I was attracted to the underlying theme of losing one's self in another reality. I'd been playing around in this arena since I started working on *Star Trek*, as well as in a pilot I produced for Fox called *Virtuality*. When I read 'Exhibit Piece' it struck me that there was an opportunity to do a show about the virtual reality technology that was just coming into being for the consumer market. I think VR is an exciting new frontier in entertainment but, as always, we tend to create new devices first and then think about their societal ramifications later. The more I thought about a story where the central character lost himself (or herself) in another world, the more I realized that I could take the core idea of this short and expand it out into a bigger exploration of both VR and the nature of reality itself. I've found this happens over and over in the PKD universe – interesting and provocative themes buried within his work that are still relevant to our lives many years after they were originally written. Very little remains of this story in the show, but the heart, and perhaps more importantly, the *brains* behind the episode originate in this tale.

EXHIBIT PIECE

'That's a strange suit you have on,' the robot pubtrans driver observed. It slid back its door and came to rest at the curb. 'What are the little round things?'

'Those are buttons,' George Miller explained. 'They are partly functional, partly ornamental. This is an archaic suit of the twentieth century. I wear it because of the nature of my employment.'

He paid the robot, grabbed up his briefcase, and hurried along the ramp to the History Agency. The main building was already open for the day; robed men and women wandered everywhere. Miller entered a PRIVATE lift, squeezed between two immense controllers from the pre-Christian division, and in a moment was on his way to his own level, the Middle Twentieth Century.

'Gorning,' he murmured, as Controller Fleming met him at the atomic engine exhibit.

'Gorning,' Fleming responded brusquely. 'Look here, Miller. Let's have this out once and for all. What if everyone dressed like you? The Government sets up strict rules for dress. Can't you forget your damn anachronisms once in a while? What in God's name is that thing in your hand? It looks like a squashed Jurassic lizard.'

'This is an alligator hide briefcase,' Miller explained. 'I carry my study spools in it. The briefcase was an authority symbol of the managerial class of the later twentieth century.' He unzipped the briefcase. 'Try to understand, Fleming. By accustoming myself to everyday objects of my research period I transform my relation from mere intellectual curiosity to genuine empathy. You have frequently noticed I pronounce certain words oddly. The accent is that of an American businessman of the Eisenhower administration. Dig me?'

'Eh?' Fleming muttered.

'*Dig me* was a twentieth century expression.' Miller laid out his study spools on his desk. 'Was there anything you wanted? If not I'll begin today's work. I've uncovered fascinating evidence to indicate that although twentieth-century Americans laid their own floor tiles, they did not weave their own clothing. I wish to alter my exhibits on this matter.'

'There's no fanatic like an academician,' Fleming grated. 'You're two hundred years behind times. Immersed in your relics and artifacts. Your damn authentic replicas of discarded trivia.'

'I love my work,' Miller answered mildly.

'Nobody complains about your work. But there are other things than work. You're a political-social unit here in this society. Take warning, Miller! The Board has reports on your eccentricities. They approve devotion to work . . .' His eyes narrowed significantly. 'But you go too far.'

'My first loyalty is to my art,' Miller said.

'Your what? What does that mean?'

'A twentieth-century term.' There was undisguised superiority on Miller's face. 'You're nothing but a minor bureaucrat in a vast machine. You're a function of an impersonal cultural totality. You have no standards of your own. In the twentieth century men had personal standards of workmanship. Artistic craft. Pride of accomplishment. These words mean nothing to you. You have no soul—another concept from the golden days of the twentieth century when men were free and could speak their minds.'

'Beware, Miller!' Fleming blanched nervously and lowered his voice. 'You damn scholars. Come up out of your tapes and face reality. You'll get us all in trouble, talking this way. Idolize the past, if you want. But remember—it's gone and buried. Times change. Society progresses.' He gestured impatiently at the exhibits that occupied the level. 'That's only an imperfect replica.'

'You impugn my research?' Miller was seething. 'This exhibit is absolutely accurate! I correct it to all new data. There isn't anything I don't know about the twentieth century.'

Fleming shook his head. 'It's no use.' He turned and stalked wearily off the level, on to the descent ramp.

Miller straightened his collar and bright hand-painted necktie. He smoothed down his blue pinstripe coat, expertly lit a pipeful of two-century-old tobacco, and returned to his spools.

Why didn't Fleming leave him alone? Fleming, the officious representative of the great hierarchy that spread like a sticky gray web over the whole planet. Into each industrial, professional, and residential unit. Ah, the freedom of the twentieth century! He slowed his tape scanner a moment, and a dreamy look slid over his features. The exciting age of virility and individuality, when men were men . . .

It was just about then, just as he was settling deep in the beauty of his research, that he heard the inexplicable sounds. They came from the center of his exhibit, from within the intricate, carefully regulated interior.

Somebody was in his exhibit.

He could hear them back there, back in the depths. Somebody or something had gone past the safety barrier set up to keep the public out. Miller snapped off his tape scanner and got slowly to his feet. He was shaking all over as he moved cautiously toward the exhibit. He killed the barrier and climbed the railing on to a concrete pavement. A few curious visitors blinked, as the small, oddly dressed man crept among the authentic replicas of the twentieth century that made up the exhibit and disappeared within.

Breathing hard, Miller advanced up the pavement and on to a carefully tended gravel path. Maybe it was one of the other theorists, a minion of the Board, snooping around looking for something with which to discredit him. An inaccuracy here—a trifling error of no consequence there. Sweat came out of his forehead; anger became terror. To his right was a flower bed. Paul Scarlet roses and low-growing pansies. Then the moist green lawn. The gleaming white garage, with its door half up. The sleek rear of a 1954 Buick—and then the house itself.

He'd have to be careful. If it *was* somebody from the Board he'd be up against official hierarchy. Maybe it was somebody big. Maybe even Edwin Carnap, President of the Board, the highest ranking official in the N'York branch of the World Directorate. Shakily, Miller climbed the three cement steps. Now he was on the porch of the twentieth-century house that made up the center of the exhibit.

It was a nice little house; if he had lived back in those days he would have wanted one of his own. Three bedrooms, a ranch style California bungalow. He pushed open the front door and entered the living room. Fireplace at one end. Dark wine-colored carpets. Modern couch and easy chair. Low hardwood glass-topped coffee table. Copper ashtrays. A cigarette lighter and a stack of magazines. Sleek plastic and steel floor lamps. A bookcase. Television set. Picture window overlooking the front garden. He crossed the room to the hall.

The house was amazingly complete. Below his feet the floor furnace radiated a faint aura of warmth. He peered into the first bedroom. A woman's boudoir. Silk bedcover. White starched sheets. Heavy drapes. A vanity table. Bottles and jars. Huge round mirror. Clothes visible within the closet. A dressing gown thrown over the back of a chair. Slippers. Nylon hose carefully placed at the foot of the bed.

Miller moved down the hall and peered into the next room. Brightly painted wallpaper: clowns and elephants and tightrope walkers. The children's room. Two little beds for the two boys. Model airplanes. A dresser with a radio on it, pair of combs, school books, pennants, a No Parking sign, snapshots stuck in the mirror. A postage stamp album.

Nobody there, either.

Miller peered in the modern bathroom, even in the yellow-tiled shower. He passed through the dining room, glanced down the basement stairs where the washing machine and dryer were. Then he opened the back door and examined the back yard. A lawn, and the incinerator. A couple of small trees and then the three-dimensional projected backdrop of other houses receding off into incredibly convincing blue hills. And still no one. The yard was empty—deserted. He closed the door and started back.

From the kitchen came laughter.

A woman's laugh. The clink of spoons and dishes. And smells. It took him a moment to identify them, scholar that he was. Bacon and coffee. And hot cakes. Somebody was eating breakfast. A twentieth-century breakfast.

He made his way down the hall, past a man's bedroom, shoes and clothing strewn about, to the entrance of the kitchen.

A handsome late-thirtyish woman and two teenage boys were sitting around the little chrome and plastic breakfast table. They had finished eating; the two boys were fidgeting impatiently. Sunlight filtered through the window over the sink. The electric clock read half past eight. The radio was chirping merrily in the corner. A big pot of black coffee rested in the center of the table, surrounded by empty plates and milk glasses and silverware.

The woman had on a white blouse and checkered tweed skirt. Both boys wore faded blue jeans, sweatshirts, and tennis shoes. As yet they hadn't noticed him. Miller stood frozen at the doorway, while laughter and small talk bubbled around him.

'You'll have to ask your father,' the woman was saying, with mock sternness. 'Wait until he comes back.'

'He already said we could,' one of the boys protested.

'Well, ask him again.'

'He's always grouchy in the morning.'

'Not today. He had a good night's sleep. His hay fever didn't bother him. The new anti-hist the doctor gave him.' She glanced up at the clock. 'Go see what's keeping him, Don. He'll be late for work.'

'He was looking for the newspaper.' One of the boys pushed back his chair and got up. 'It missed the porch again and fell in the flowers.' He turned towards the door, and Miller found himself confronting him face to face. Briefly, the observation flashed through his mind that the boy looked familiar. Damn familiar—like somebody he knew, only younger. He tensed himself for the impact, as the boy abruptly halted.

'Gee,' the boy said. 'You scared me.'

The woman glanced quickly up at Miller. 'What are you doing out there, George?' she demanded. 'Come on back in here and finish you coffee.'

Miller came slowly into the kitchen. The woman was finishing her coffee; both boys were on their feet and beginning to press around him.

'Didn't you tell me I could go camping over the weekend up at Russian River with the group from school?' Don demanded. 'You said I could borrow a sleeping bag from the gym because the one I had you gave to the Salvation Army because you were allergic to the kapok in it.'

'Yeah,' Miller muttered uncertainly. Don. That was the boy's name. And his brother, Ted. But how did he know that? At the table the woman had got up and was collecting the dirty dishes to carry over to the sink. 'They said you already promised them,' she said over her shoulder. The dishes clattered into the sink and she began sprinkling soap flakes over them. 'But you remember that time they wanted to drive the car and the way they said it, you'd think they had got your okay. And they hadn't, of course.'

Miller sank weakly down at the table. Aimlessly, he fooled with his pipe. He set it down in the copper ashtray and examined the cuff of his coat. What was happening? His head spun. He got up abruptly and hurried to the window, over the sink.

Houses, streets. The distant hills beyond the town. The sights and sounds of people. The three dimensional projected backdrop was utterly convincing; or was it the projected backdrop? How could he be sure. *What was happening?*

'George, what's the matter?' Marjorie asked, as she tied a pink plastic apron around her waist and began running hot water in the sink. 'You better get the car out and get started to work. Weren't you saying last night old man Davidson was shouting about employees being late for work and standing around the water cooler talking and having a good time on company time?'

Davidson. The word stuck in Miller's mind. He knew it, of course. A clear picture leaped up; a tall, white-haired old man, thin and stern. Vest and pocket watch. And the whole office, United Electronic Supply. The twelve-story building in downtown San Francisco. The newspaper and cigar stand in the lobby. The honking cars. Jammed parking lots. The elevator, packed with bright-eyed secretaries, tight sweaters and perfume.

He wandered out of the kitchen, through the hall, past his own bedroom, his wife's, and into the living room. The front door was open and he stepped out on to the porch.

The air was cool and sweet. It was a bright April morning. The lawns were still wet. Cars moved down Virginia Street, towards Shattuck Avenue. Early morning commuting traffic, businessmen on their way to work. Across the street Earl Kelly cheerfully waved his Oakland Tribune as he hurried down the pavement towards the bus stop.

A long way off Miller could see the Bay Bridge, Yerba Buena Island, and Treasure Island. Beyond that was San Francisco itself. In a few minutes he'd be shooting across the bridge in his Buick, on his way to the office. Along with thousands of other businessmen in blue pinstripe suits.

Ted pushed past him and out on the porch. 'Then it's okay? You don't care if we go camping?'

Miller licked his dry lips. 'Ted, listen to me. There's something strange.'

'Like what?'

'I don't know.' Miller wandered nervously around on the porch. 'This is Friday, isn't it?'

'Sure.'

'I thought it was.' But how did he know it was Friday? How did he know anything? But of course it was Friday. A long hard week—old man Davidson breathing down his neck. Wednesday, especially, when the General Electric order was slowed down because of a strike.

'Let me ask you something,' Miller said to his son. 'This morning—I left the kitchen to get the newspaper.'

Ted nodded. 'Yeah. So?'

'I got up and went out of the room. *How long was I gone?* Not long, was I?' He searched for words, but his mind was a maze of disjointed thoughts. 'I was sitting at the breakfast table with you all, and then I got up and went to look for the paper. Right? And then I came back in. Right?' His voice rose desperately. 'I got up and shaved and dressed this morning. I ate breakfast. Hot cakes and coffee. Bacon. *Right?*'

'Right,' Ted agreed. 'So?'

'Like I always do.'

'We only have hot cakes on Friday.'

Miller nodded slowly. 'That's right. Hot cakes on Friday. Because your uncle Frank eats with us Saturday and Sunday and he can't stand hot cakes, so we stopped having them on weekends. Frank is Marjorie's brother. He was in the Marines in the First World War. He was a corporal.'

'Good-bye,' Ted said, as Don came out to join him. 'We'll see you this evening.'

School books clutched, the boys sauntered off towards the big modern high school in the center of Berkeley.

Miller re-entered the house and automatically began searching the closet for his briefcase. Where was it? Damn it, he needed it. The whole Throckmorton account was in it; Davidson would be yelling his head off if he left it anywhere, like in the True Blue Cafeteria that time they were all celebrating the Yankees' winning the series. Where the hell was it?

He straightened up slowly, as memory came. Of course. He had left it by his work desk, where he had tossed it after taking out the research tapes. While Fleming was talking to him. Back at the History Agency.

He joined his wife in the kitchen. 'Look,' he said huskily. 'Marjorie, I think maybe I won't go down to the office this morning.'

Marjorie spun in alarm. 'George, is anything wrong?'

'I'm—completely confused.'

'Your hay fever again?'

'No. My mind. What's the name of that psychiatrist the PTA recommended when Mrs Bentley's kid had that fit?' He searched his disorganized brain. 'Grunberg, I think. In the Medical-Dental building.' He moved towards the door. 'I'll drop by and see him. Something's wrong—really wrong. And I don't know what it is.'

Adam Grunberg was a large heavy-set man in his late forties, with curly brown hair and horn-rimmed glasses. After Miller had finished, Grunberg cleared his throat, brushed at the sleeve of his Brooks Bros' suit, and asked thoughtfully, 'Did anything happen while you were out looking for the newspaper? Any sort of accident? You might try going over that part in detail. You got up from the breakfast table, went out on the porch, and started looking around in the bushes. And then what?'

Miller rubbed his forehead vaguely. 'I don't know. It's all confused. I don't remember looking for any newspaper. I remember coming back in the house. Then it gets clear. But before that it's all tied up with the History Agency and my quarrel with Fleming.'

'What was that again about your briefcase? Go over that.'

'Fleming said it looked like a squashed Jurassic lizard. And I said—'

'No. I mean, about looking for it in the closet and not finding it.'

'I looked in the closet and it wasn't there, of course. It's sitting beside my desk at the History Agency. On the Twentieth Century level. By my exhibits.' A strange expression crossed Miller's face. 'Good God, Grunberg.

You realize this may be nothing but an *exhibit*? You and everybody else—maybe you're not real. Just pieces of this exhibit.'

'That wouldn't be very pleasant for us, would it?' Grunberg said, with a faint smile.

'People in dreams are always secure until the dreamer wakes up,' Miller retorted.

'So you're dreaming me,' Grunberg laughed tolerantly. 'I suppose I should thank you.'

'I'm not here because I especially like you. I'm here because I can't stand Fleming and the whole History Agency.'

Grunberg protested. 'This Fleming. Are you aware of thinking about him before you went out looking for the newspaper?'

Miller got to his feet and paced around the luxurious office, between the leather-covered chairs and the huge mahogany desk. 'I want to face this thing. I'm an exhibit. An artificial replica of the past. Fleming said something like this would happen to me.'

'Sit down, Mr Miller,' Grunberg said, in a gentle but commanding voice. When Miller had taken his chair again, Grunberg continued, 'I understand what you say. You have a general feeling that everything around you is unreal. A sort of stage.'

'An exhibit.'

'Yes, an exhibit in a museum.'

'In the N'York History Agency. Level R, the Twentieth Century level.'

'And in addition to this general feeling of—insubstantiality, there are specific projected memories of persons and places beyond this world. Another realm in which this one is contained. Perhaps I should say, the reality within which this is only a sort of shadow world.'

'This world doesn't look shadowy to me.' Miller struck the leather arm of the chair savagely. 'This world is completely real. That's what's wrong. I came in to investigate the noises and now I can't get back out. Good God, do I have to wander around this replica the rest of my life?'

'You know, of course, that your feeling is common to most of mankind. Especially during periods of great tension. Where—by the way—was the newspaper? Did you find it?'

'As far as I'm concerned—'

'Is that a source of irritation with you? I see you react strongly to a mention of the newspaper.'

Miller shook his head wearily. 'Forget it.'

'Yes, a trifle. The paperboy carelessly throws the newspaper in the bushes, not on the porch. It makes you angry. It happens again and again. Early in the day, just as you're starting to work. It seems to symbolize in a small way the whole petty frustrations and defeats of your job. Your whole life.'

'Personally, I don't give a damn about the newspaper.' Miller examined his wristwatch. 'I'm going—it's almost noon. Old man Davidson will be yelling his head off if I'm not at the office by—' He broke off. 'There it is again.'

'There what is?'

'All this!' Miller gestured impatiently out the window. 'This whole place. This damn world. This *exhibition*.'

'I have a thought,' Doctor Grunberg said slowly. 'I'll put it to you for what it's worth. Feel free to reject it if it doesn't fit.' He raised his shrewd, professional eyes. 'Ever see kids playing with rocket ships?'

'Lord,' Miller said wretchedly. 'I've seen commercial rocket freighters hauling cargo between Earth and Jupiter, landing at La Guardia Spaceport.'

Grunberg smiled slightly. 'Follow me through on this. A question. Is it job tension?'

'What do you mean?'

'It would be nice,' Grunberg said blandly, 'to live in the world of tomorrow. With robots and rocket ships to do all the work. You could just sit back and take it easy. No worries, no cares. No frustrations.'

'My position in the History Agency has plenty of cares and frustrations.' Miller rose abruptly. 'Look, Grunberg. Either this is an exhibit on R level of the History Agency, or I'm a middle-class businessman with an escape fantasy. Right now I can't decide which. One minute I think this is real, and the next minute—'

'We can decide easily,' Grunberg said.

'How?'

'You were looking for the newspaper. Down the path, on to the lawn. *Where did it happen?* Was it on the path? On the porch? Try to remember.'

'I don't have to try. I was still on the pavement. I had just jumped over the rail past the safety screens.'

'On the pavement. Then go back there. Find the exact place.'

'Why?'

'So you can prove to yourself there's nothing on the other side.'

Miller took a deep slow breath. 'Suppose there is?'

'There can't be. You said yourself: only one of the worlds can be real. This world is real—' Grunberg thumped his massive mahogany desk. 'Ergo, you won't find anything on the other side.'

'Yes,' Miller said, after a moment's silence. A peculiar expression cut across his face and stayed there. 'You've found the mistake.'

'What mistake?' Grunberg was puzzled. 'What—'

Miller moved towards the door of the office. 'I'm beginning to get it. I've been putting up a false question. Trying to decide which world is real.' He grinned humorlessly back at Doctor Grunberg. 'They're both real, of course.'

He grabbed a taxi and headed back to the house. No one was home. The boys were in school and Marjorie had gone downtown to shop. He waited indoors until he was sure nobody was watching along the street, and then started down the path to the pavement.

He found the spot without any trouble. There was a faint shimmer in the air, a weak place just at the edge of the parking strip. Through it he could see faint shapes.

He was right. There it was—complete and real. As real as the pavement under him.

A long metallic bar was cut off by the edges of the circle. He recognized it; the safety railing he had leaped over to enter the exhibit. Beyond it was the safety screen system. Turned off, of course. And beyond that, the rest of the level and the far walls of the History building.

He took a cautious step into the weak haze. It shimmered around him, misty and oblique. The shapes beyond became clearer. A moving figure in a dark blue robe. Some curious person examining the exhibits. The figure moved on and was lost. He could see his own work desk now. His tape scanner and heaps of study spools. Beside the desk was his briefcase, exactly where he had expected it.

While he was considering stepping over the railing to get the briefcase, Fleming appeared.

Some inner instinct made Miller step back through the weak spot, as Fleming approached. Maybe it was the expression on Fleming's face. In any case, Miller was back and standing firmly on the concrete pavement, when Fleming halted just beyond the juncture, face red, lips twisted with indignation.

'Miller,' he said thickly. 'Come out of there.'

Miller laughed. 'Be a good fellow, Fleming. Toss me my briefcase. It's that strange looking thing over by the desk. I showed it to you—remember?'

'Stop playing games and listen to me!' Fleming snapped. 'This is serious. *Carnap knows*, I had to inform him.'

'Good for you. The loyal bureaucrat.'

Miller bent over to light his pipe. He inhaled and puffed a great cloud of gray tobacco smoke through the weak spot, out into the R level. Fleming coughed and retreated.

'What's that stuff?' he demanded.

'Tobacco. One of the things they have around here. Very common substance in the twentieth century. You wouldn't know about that—your period is the second century, B.C. The Hellenistic world. I don't know how well you'd like that. They didn't have very good plumbing back there. Life expectancy was damn short.'

'What are you talking about?'

'In comparison, the life expectancy of *my* research period is quite high. And you should see the bathroom I've got. Yellow tile. And a shower. We don't have anything like that at the Agency leisure-quarters.'

Fleming grunted sourly. 'In other words, you're going to stay in there.'

'It's a pleasant place,' Miller said easily. 'Of course, my position is better than average. Let me describe it for you. I have an attractive wife: marriage is permitted, even sanctioned in this era. I have two fine kids—both boys—who are going up to the Russian River this weekend. They live with me and my wife—we have complete custody of them. The State has no power of that, yet. I have a brand new Buick—'

'Illusions,' Fleming spat. 'Psychotic delusions.'

'Are you sure?'

'You damn fool! I always knew you were too ego-recessive to face reality. You and your anachronistic retreats. Sometimes I'm ashamed I'm a theoretician. I wish I had gone into engineering.' Fleming's lips twitched. 'You're insane, you know. You're standing in the middle of an artificial exhibit, which is owned by the History Agency, a bundle of plastic and wire and struts. A replica of a past age. An imitation. And you'd rather be there than in the real world.'

'Strange,' Miller said thoughtfully. 'Seems to me I've heard the same thing very recently. You don't know a Doctor Grunberg, do you? A psychiatrist.'

Without formality, Director Carnap arrived with his company of assistants and experts. Fleming quickly retreated. Miller found himself facing one of the most powerful figures of the twenty-second century. He grinned and held out his hand.

'You insane imbecile,' Carnap rumbled. 'Get out of there before we drag you out. If we have to do that, you're through. You know what they do with advanced psychotics. It'll be euthanasia for you. I'll give you one last chance to come out of that fake exhibit—'

'Sorry,' Miller said. 'It's not an exhibit.'

Carnap's heavy face registered sudden surprise. For a brief instant his massive pose vanished. 'You still try to maintain—'

'This is a time gate,' Miller said quietly. 'You can't get me out, Carnap. You can't reach me. I'm in the past, two hundred years back. I've crossed back to a previous exist-ence-coordinate. I found a bridge and escaped from your continuum to this. And there's nothing you can do about it.'

Carnap and his experts huddled together in a quick tech-nical conference. Miller waited patiently. He had plenty of time; he had decided not to show up at the office until Monday.

After a while Carnap approached the juncture again, being careful not to step over the safety rail. 'An interesting theory, Miller. That's the strange part about psychotics. They rationalize their delusions into a logical system. *A priori*, your concept stands up well. It's internally consistent. Only—'

'Only what?'

'Only it doesn't happen to be true.' Carnap had regained his confidence; he seemed to be enjoying the interchange. 'You think you're really back in the past. Yes, this exhibit is extremely accurate. Your work has always been good. The authenticity of detail is unequalled by any of the other exhibits.'

'I tried to do my work well,' Miller murmured.

'You wore archaic clothing and affected archaic speech mannerisms. You did everything possible to throw yourself back. You devoted yourself to your work.' Carnap tapped the safety railing with his fingernail. 'It would be a shame, Miller. A terrible shame to demolish such an authentic replica.'

'I see your point,' Miller said, after a time. 'I agree with you, certainly. I've been very proud of my work—I'd hate to see it all torn down. But that really won't do you any good. All you'll succeed in doing is closing the time gate.'

'You're sure?'

'Of course. The exhibit is only a bridge, a link with the past. I passed *through* the exhibit, but I'm not there now. I'm beyond the exhibit.' He grinned tightly. 'Your demolition can't reach me. But seal me off, if you want. I don't think I'll be wanting to come back. I wish you could see this side, Carnap. It's a nice place here. Freedom, opportunity. Limited government, responsible to the people. If you don't like a job here you quit. There's no euthanasia, here. Come on over. I'll introduce you to my wife.'

'We'll get you,' Carnap said. 'And all your psychotic figments along with you.'

'I doubt if any of my "psychotic figments" are worried. Grunberg wasn't. I don't think Marjorie is—'

'We've already begun demolition preparations,' Carnap said calmly. 'We'll do it piece by piece, not all at once. So you may have the opportunity to appreciate the scientific and—*artistic* way we take your imaginary world apart.'

'You're wasting your time,' Miller said. He turned and walked off, down the pavement, to the gravel path and up on to the front porch of the house.

In the living room he threw himself down in the easy chair and snapped on the television set. Then he went to the kitchen and got a can of ice cold beer. He carried it happily back into the safe, comfortable living room.

As he was seating himself in front of the television set he noticed something rolled up on the low coffee table.

He grinned wryly. It was the morning newspaper, which he had looked so hard for. Marjorie had brought it in with the milk, as usual. And of course forgotten to tell him. He yawned contentedly and reached over to pick it up. Confidently, he unfolded it—and read the big black headlines.

RUSSIA REVEALS COBALT BOMB
TOTAL WORLD DESTRUCTION AHEAD

Introduction by Jack Thorne

Story & Script title: The Commuter

Jack Thorne is a five time BAFTA winning writer and producer known for acclaimed television shows such as The Last Panthers and National Treasure, original features The Scouting Book For Boys and War Book and he adapted Nick Hornby's A Long Way Down. Jack's plays have been staged internationally and include the West End play Harry Potter & The Cursed Child and Woyzeck starring John Boyega.

What's to say about PK Dick that hasn't been said? I'm sure there are a list of people in this book praising his vision and ability to transport the reader to faraway places in a blink of an eye. His imagination is so full, so thorough. As someone who read a lot of science-fiction there is always a difference between those writers who have ideas, and those who build worlds. PKD builds universes.

But what I most admire about him – and what drew me to *The Commuter* – is that he always finds the ordinary in the extraordinary. None of his characters are superheroes in waiting, rather they are Ordinary Joes – who have been given a glance through a window and respond accordingly. They don't suddenly change who they are – but as the world transforms so they transform within it.

★

My Grandad spent his life as a ticket clerk at Euston Station in London. So *The Commuter* immediately drew me in. The idea that he'd be given a chance to see new possibilities. To see places that didn't exist – but could exist. To see somewhere which he could love and which allowed the possibility of escape from his life. I don't want to say too much more – because I don't want to spoil the twists and turns of this story – but as always with PKD's work it ends up asking profound questions about what as humans we want. And what we should get.

I've spent the last year immersed in this story – and there are still questions I'm having to ask about it as I reread it. I hope you find it as beautiful as I do.

THE COMMUTER

The little fellow was tired. He pushed his way slowly through the throng of people, across the lobby of the station, to the ticket window. He waited his turn impatiently, fatigue showing in his drooping shoulders, his sagging brown coat.

'Next,' Ed Jacobson, the ticket seller, rasped.

The little fellow tossed a five dollar bill on the counter. 'Give me a new commute book. Used up the old one.' He peered past Jacobson at the wall clock. 'Lord, is it really that late?'

Jacobson accepted the five dollars. 'OK, mister. One commute book. Where to?'

'Macon Heights,' the little fellow stated.

'Macon Heights.' Jacobson consulted his board. 'Macon Heights. There isn't any such place.'

The little man's face hardened in suspicion. 'You trying to be funny?'

'Mister, there isn't any Macon Heights. I can't sell you a ticket unless there is such a place.'

'What do you mean? I live there!'

'I don't care. I've been selling tickets for six years and there is no such place.'

The little man's eyes popped with astonishment. 'But I have a home there. I go there every night. I—'

'Here.' Jacobson pushed him the chart board. 'You find it.'

The little man pulled the board over to one side. He studied it frantically, his finger trembling as he went down the list of towns.

'Find it?' Jacobson demanded, resting his arms on the counter. 'It's not there, is it?'

The little man shook his head, dazed. 'I don't understand. It doesn't make sense. Something must be wrong. There certainly must be—'

Suddenly he vanished. The board fell to the cement floor. The little fellow was gone—winked out of existence.

'Holy Caesar's Ghost,' Jacobson gasped. His mouth opened and closed. There was only the board lying on the cement floor.

The little man had ceased to exist.

'What then?' Bob Paine asked.

'I went around and picked up the board.'

'He was really gone?'

'He was gone, all right.' Jacobson mopped his forehead. 'I wish you had been around. Like a light he went out. Completely. No sound. No motion.'

Paine lit a cigarette, leaning back in his chair. 'Had you ever seen him before?'

'No.'

'What time of day was it?'

'Just about now. About five.' Jacobson moved toward the ticket window. 'Here comes a bunch of people.'

'Macon Heights.' Paine turned the pages of the State city guide. 'No listing in any of the books. If he reappears I want to talk to him. Get him inside the office.'

'Sure. I don't want to have nothing to do with him. It isn't natural.' Jacobson turned to the window. 'Yes, lady.'

'Two round trip tickets to Lewisburg.'

Paine stubbed his cigarette out and lit another. 'I keep feeling I've heard the name before.' He got up and wandered over to the wall map. 'But it isn't listed.'

'There is no listing because there is no such place,' Jacobson said. 'You think I could stand here daily, selling one ticket after another, and not know?' He turned back to his window. 'Yes, sir.'

'I'd like a commute book to Macon Heights,' the little fellow said, glancing nervously at the clock on the wall. 'And hurry it up.'

Jacobson closed his eyes. He hung on tight. When he opened his eyes again the little fellow was still there. Small wrinkled face. Thinning hair. Glasses. Tired, slumped coat.

Jacobson turned and moved across the office to Paine. 'He's back.' Jacobson swallowed, his face pale. 'It's him again.'

Paine's eyes flickered. 'Bring him right in.'

Jacobson nodded and returned to the window. 'Mister,' he said, 'could you please come inside?' He indicated the door. 'The vice-president would like to see you for a moment.'

The little man's face darkened. 'What's up? The train's about to take off.' Grumbling under his breath, he pushed the door open and entered the office. 'This sort of thing has never happened before. It's certainly getting hard to purchase a commute book. If I miss the train I'm going to hold your company—'

'Sit down,' Paine said, indicating the chair across from his desk. 'You're the gentleman who wants a commute book to Macon Heights?'

'Is there something strange about that? What's the matter with all of you? Why can't you sell me a commute book like you always do?'

'Like—like we *always* do?'

The little man held himself in check with great effort. 'Last December my wife and I moved out to Macon Heights. I've been riding your train ten times a week, twice a day, for six months. Every month I buy a new commute book.'

Paine leaned toward him. 'Exactly which one of our trains do you take, Mr—'

'Critchet. Ernest Critchet. The B train. Don't you know your own schedules?'

'The B train?' Paine consulted a B train chart, running his pencil along it. No Macon Heights was listed. 'How long is the trip? How long does it take?'

'Exactly forty-nine minutes.' Critchet looked up at the wall clock. 'If I ever get on it.'

Paine calculated mentally. Forty-nine minutes. About thirty miles from the city. He got up and crossed to the big wall map.

'What's wrong?' Critchet asked with marked suspicion.

Paine drew a thirty-mile circle on the map. The circle crossed a number of towns, but none of them was Macon Heights. And on the B line there was nothing at all.

'What sort of place is Macon Heights?' Paine asked. 'How many people, would you say?'

'I don't know. Five thousand, maybe. I spend most of my time in the city. I'm a bookkeeper over at Bradshaw Insurance.'

'Is Macon Heights a fairly new place?'

'It's modern enough. We have a little two-bedroom house, a couple years old.' Critchet stirred restlessly. 'How about a commute book?'

'I'm afraid,' Paine said slowly, 'I can't sell you a commute book.'

'What? Why not?'

'We don't have any service to Macon Heights.'

Critchet leaped up. 'What do you mean?'

'There's no such place. Look at the map yourself.'

Critchet gaped, his face working. Then he turned angrily to the wall map, glaring at it intently.

'This is a curious situation, Mr Critchet,' Paine murmured. 'It isn't on the map, and the State city directory doesn't list it. We have no schedule that includes it. There are no commute books made up for it. We don't—'

He broke off. Critchet had vanished. One moment he was there, studying the wall map. The next moment he was gone. Vanished. Puffed out.

'Jacobson!' Paine barked. 'He's gone!'

Jacobson's eyes grew large. Sweat stood out on his forehead. 'So he is,' he murmured.

Paine was deep in thought, gazing at the empty spot Ernest Critchet had occupied. 'Something's going on,' he muttered. 'Something damn strange.' Abruptly he grabbed his overcoat and headed for the door.

'Don't leave me alone!' Jacobson begged.

'If you need me I'll be at Laura's apartment. The number's some place in my desk.'

'This is no time for games with girls.'

Paine pushed open the door to the lobby. 'I doubt,' he said grimly, 'if this is a game.'

Paine climbed the stairs to Laura Nichols' apartment two at a time. He leaned on the buzzer until the door opened.

'Bob!' Laura blinked in surprise. 'To what do I owe this—'

Paine pushed past her, inside the apartment. 'Hope I'm not interrupting anything.'

'No, but—'

'Big doings. I'm going to need some help. Can I count on you?'

'On me?' Laura closed the door after him. Her attractively furnished apartment lay in half shadow. At the end of the deep green couch a single table lamp burned. The heavy drapes were pulled. The phonograph was on low in the corner.

'Maybe I'm going crazy.' Paine threw himself down on the luxuriant green couch. 'That's what I want to find out.'

'How can I help?' Laura came languidly over, her arms folded, a cigarette between her lips. She shook her long hair back out of her eyes. 'Just what did you have in mind?'

Paine grinned at the girl appreciatively. 'You'll be surprised. I want you to go downtown tomorrow morning bright and early and—'

'Tomorrow morning! I have a job, remember? And the office starts a whole new string of reports this week.'

'The hell with that. Take the morning off. Go downtown to the main library. If you can't get the information there, go over to the county courthouse and start looking through the back tax records. Keep looking until you find it.'

'It? Find what?'

Paine lit a cigarette thoughtfully. 'Mention of a place called Macon Heights. I know I've heard the name before. Years ago. Got the picture? Go through the old atlases. Old newspapers in the reading room. Old magazines. Reports. City proposals. Propositions before the State legislature.'

Laura sat down slowly on the arm of the couch. 'Are you kidding?'

'No.'

'How far back?'

'Maybe ten years—if necessary.'

'Good Lord! I might have to—'

'Stay there until you find it.' Paine got up abruptly. 'I'll see you later.'

'You're leaving. You're not taking me out to dinner?'

'Sorry.' Paine moved toward the door. 'I'll be busy. Real busy.'

'Doing what?'

'Visiting Macon Heights.'

★

Outside the train endless fields stretched off, broken by an occasional farm building. Bleak telephone poles jutted up toward the evening sky.

Paine glanced at his wristwatch. Not far, now. The train passed through a small town. A couple of gas stations, road-side stands, television store. It stopped at the station, brakes grinding. Lewisburg. A few commuters got off, men in overcoats with evening papers. The doors slammed and the train started up.

Paine settled back against his seat, deep in thought. Critchet had vanished while looking at the wall map. He had vanished the first time when Jacobson showed him the chart board . . . When he had been shown there was no such place as Macon Heights. Was there some sort of clue there? The whole thing was unreal, dreamlike.

Paine peered out. He was almost there—if there were such a place. Outside the train the brown fields stretched off endlessly. Hills and level fields. Telephone poles. Cars racing along the State highway, tiny black specks hurrying through the twilight.

But no sign of Macon Heights.

The train roared on its way. Paine consulted his watch. Fifty-one minutes had passed. And he had seen nothing. Nothing but fields.

He walked up the car and sat down beside the conductor, a white-haired old gentleman. 'Ever hear of a place called Macon Heights?' Paine asked.

'No, sir.'

Paine showed his identification. 'You're sure you never heard of any place by that name?'

'Positive, Mr Paine.'

'How long have you been on this run?'

'Eleven years, Mr Paine.'

Paine rode on until the next stop, Jacksonville. He got off and transferred to a B train heading back to the city. The sun had set. The sky was almost black. Dimly, he could make out the scenery out there beyond the window.

He tensed, holding his breath. One minute to go. Forty seconds. Was there anything? Level fields. Bleak telephone poles. A barren, wasted landscape between towns.

Between? The train rushed on, hurtling through the gloom. Paine gazed out fixedly. Was there something out there? Something beside the fields?

Above the fields a long mass of translucent smoke lay stretched out. A homogeneous mass, extended for almost a mile. What was it? Smoke from the engine? But the engine was diesel. From a truck along the highway? A brush fire? None of the fields looked burned.

Suddenly the train began to slow. Paine was instantly alert. The train was stopping, coming to a halt. The brakes screeched, the cars lurched from side to side. Then silence.

Across the aisle a tall man in a light coat got to his feet, put his hat on, and moved rapidly toward the door. He leaped down from the train, onto the ground. Paine watched him, fascinated. The man walked rapidly away from the train across the dark fields. He moved with purpose, heading toward the bank of gray haze.

The man rose. He was walking a foot off the ground. He turned to the right. He rose again, now—three feet off the ground. For a moment he walked parallel to the ground, still heading away from the train. Then he vanished into the bank of haze. He was gone.

Paine hurried up the aisle. But already the train had begun gathering speed. The ground moved past outside. Paine located the conductor, leaning against the wall of the car, a pudding-faced youth.

'Listen,' Paine grated. 'What was that stop!'

'Beg pardon, sir?'

'That stop! Where the hell were we?'

'We always stop there.' Slowly, the conductor reached into his coat and brought out a handful of schedules. He sorted through them and passed one to Paine. 'The B always stops at Macon Heights. Didn't you know that?'

'No!'

'It's on the schedule.' The youth raised his pulp magazine again. 'Always stops there. Always has. Always will.'

Paine tore the schedule open. It was true. Macon Heights was listed between Jacksonville and Lewisburg. Exactly thirty miles from the city.

The cloud of gray haze. The vast cloud, gaining form rapidly. As if something were coming into existence. As a matter of fact, something *was* coming into existence.

Macon Heights!

He caught Laura at her apartment the next morning. She was sitting at the coffee table in a pale pink sweater and dark slacks. Before her was a pile of notes, a pencil and eraser, and a malted milk.

'How did you make out?' Paine demanded.

'Fine. I got your information.'

'What's the story?'

'There was quite a bit of material.' She patted the sheaf of notes. 'I summed up the major parts for you.'

'Let's have the summation.'

'Seven years ago this August the county board of supervisors voted on three new suburban housing tracts to be set up outside the city. Macon Heights was one of them. There was a big debate. Most of the city merchants opposed the

new tracts. Said they would draw too much retail business
away from the city.'

'Go on.'

'There was a long fight. Finally two of the three tracts
were approved. Waterville and Cedar Groves. But not Macon
Heights.'

'I see,' Paine murmured thoughtfully.

'Macon Heights was defeated. A compromise; two tracts
instead of three. The two tracts were built up right away.
You know. We passed through Waterville one afternoon.
Nice little place.'

'But no Macon Heights.'

'No. Macon Heights was given up.'

Paine rubbed his jaw. 'That's the story, then.'

'That's the story. Do you realize I lose a whole half-day's
pay because of this? You *have* to take me out, tonight. Maybe
I should get another fellow. I'm beginning to think you're
not such a good bet.'

Paine nodded absently. 'Seven years ago.' All at once a
thought came to him. 'The vote! How close was the vote
on Macon Heights?'

Laura consulted her notes. 'The project was defeated by
a single vote.'

'A single vote. Seven years ago.' Paine moved out into
the hall. 'Thanks, honey. Things are beginning to make
sense. Lots of sense!'

He caught a cab out front. The cab raced him across the
city, toward the train station. Outside, signs and streets flashed
by. People and stores and cars.

His hunch had been correct. He *had* heard the name
before. Seven years ago. A bitter county debate on a proposed
suburban tract. Two towns approved; one defeated and
forgotten.

But now the forgotten town was coming into existence—seven years later. The town and an undetermined slice of reality along with it. *Why*? Had something changed in the past? Had an alteration occurred in some past continuum?

That seemed like the explanation. The vote had been close. Macon Heights had *almost* been approved. Maybe certain parts of the past were unstable. Maybe that particular period, seven years ago, had been critical. Maybe it had never completely 'jelled.' An odd thought: the past changing, after it had already happened.

Suddenly Paine's eyes focused. He sat up quickly. Across the street was a store sign, halfway along the block. Over a small, inconspicuous establishment. As the cab moved forward Paine peered to see.

BRADSHAW INSURANCE
[OR]
NOTARY PUBLIC

He pondered. Critchet's place of business. Did it also come and go? Had it always been there? Something about it made him uneasy.

'Hurry it up,' Paine ordered the driver. 'Let's get going.'

When the train slowed down at Macon Heights, Paine got quickly to his feet and made his way up the aisle to the door. The grinding wheels jerked to a halt and Paine leaped down onto the hot gravel siding. He looked around him.

In the afternoon sunlight, Macon Heights glittered and sparkled, its even rows of houses stretching out in all directions. In the center of the town the marquee of a theater rose up.

A theater, even. Paine headed across the track toward the town. Beyond the train station was a parking lot. He stepped up onto the lot and crossed it, following a path past a filling station and onto a sidewalk.

He came out on the main street of the town. A double row of stores stretched out ahead of him. A hardware store. Two drugstores. A dime store. A modern department store.

Paine walked along, hands in his pockets, gazing around him at Macon Heights. An apartment building stuck up, tall and fat. A janitor was washing down the front steps. Everything looked new and modern. The houses, the stores, the pavement and sidewalks. The parking meters. A brown-uniformed cop was giving a car a ticket. Trees, growing at intervals. Neatly clipped and pruned.

He passed a big supermarket. Out in front was a bin of fruit, oranges and grapes. He picked a grape and bit into it.

The grape was real, all right. A big black concord grape, sweet and ripe. Yet twenty-four hours ago there had been nothing here but a barren field.

Paine entered one of the drugstores. He leafed through some magazines and then sat down at the counter. He ordered a cup of coffee from the red-cheeked little waitress.

'This is a nice town,' Paine said, as she brought the coffee.

'Yes, isn't it?'

Paine hesitated. 'How—how long have you been working here?'

'Three months.'

'Three months?' Paine studied the buxom little blonde. 'You live here in Macon Heights?'

'Oh, yes.'

'How long?'

'A couple years, I guess.' She moved away to wait on a young soldier who had taken a stool down the counter.

Paine sat drinking his coffee and smoking, idly watching the people passing by outside. Ordinary people. Men and women, mostly women. Some had grocery bags and little wire carts. Automobiles drove slowly back and forth. A sleepy little suburban town. Modern, upper middle-class. A quality town. No slums here. Small, attractive houses. Stores with sloping grass fronts and neon signs.

Some high school kids burst into the drugstore, laughing and bumping into each other. Two girls in bright sweaters sat down next to Paine and ordered lime drinks. They chatted gaily, bits of their conversation drifting to him.

He gazed at them, pondering moodily. They were real, all right. Lipstick and red fingernails. Sweaters and armloads of school books. Hundreds of high school kids, crowding eagerly into the drugstore.

Paine rubbed his forehead wearily. It didn't seem possible. Maybe he was out of his mind. The town was *real*. Completely real. It must have always existed. A whole town couldn't rise up out of nothing; out of a cloud of gray haze. Five thousand people, houses and streets and stores.

Stores. Bradshaw Insurance.

Stabbing realization chilled him. Suddenly he understood. It was spreading. Beyond Macon Heights. Into the city. The city was changing, too. Bradshaw Insurance. Critchet's place of business.

Macon Heights couldn't exist without warping the city. They interlocked. The five thousand people came from the city. Their jobs. Their lives. The city was involved.

But how much? How much was the city changing?

Paine threw a quarter on the counter and hurried out of the drugstore, toward the train station. He had to get back to the city. Laura, the change. Was she still there? Was his *own* life safe?

Fear gripped him. Laura, all his possessions, his plans, hopes and dreams. Suddenly Macon Heights was unimportant. His own world was in jeopardy. Only one thing mattered now. He had to make sure of it; make sure his own life was still here. Untouched by the spreading circle of change that was lapping out from Macon Heights.

'Where to, buddy?' the cabdriver asked, as Paine came rushing out of the train station.

Paine gave him the address of the apartment. The cab roared out into traffic. Paine settled back nervously. Outside the window the streets and office buildings flashed past. White collar workers were already beginning to get off work, swelling out onto the sidewalks to stand in clumps at each corner.

How much had changed? He concentrated on a row of buildings. The big department store. Had that always been there? The little boot-black shop next to it. He had never noticed that before.

NORRIS HOME FURNISHINGS.

He didn't remember *that*. But how could he be sure? He felt confused. How could he tell?

The cab let him off in front of the apartment house. Paine stood for a moment, looking around him. Down at the end of the block the owner of the Italian delicatessen was out putting up the awning. Had he ever noticed a delicatessen there before?

He could not remember.

What had happened to the big meat market across the street? There was nothing but neat little houses; older houses that looked like they'd been there plenty long. Had a meat market ever been there? The houses *looked* solid.

In the next block the striped pole of a barbershop glittered. Had there always been a barbershop there?

Maybe it had always been there. Maybe, and maybe not. Everything was shifting. New things were coming into existence, others going away. The past was altering, and memory was tied to the past. How could he trust his memory? How could he be sure?

Terror gripped him. Laura. His world . . .

Paine raced up the front steps and pushed open the door of the apartment house. He hurried up the carpeted stairs to the second floor. The door of the apartment was unlocked. He pushed it open and entered, his heart in his mouth, praying silently.

The living room was dark and silent. The shades were half pulled. He glanced around wildly. The light blue couch, magazines on its arms. The low blond-oak table. The television set. But the room was empty.

'Laura!' he gasped.

Laura hurried from the kitchen, eyes wide with alarm. 'Bob! what are you doing home? Is anything the matter?'

Paine relaxed, sagging with relief. 'Hello, honey.' He kissed her, holding her tight against him. She was warm and substantial; completely real. 'No, nothing's wrong. Everything's fine.'

'Are you sure?'

'I'm sure.' Paine took off his coat shakily and dropped it over the back of the couch. He wandered around the room, examining things, his confidence returning. His familiar blue couch, cigarette burns on its arms. His ragged footstool. His desk where he did his work at night. His fishing rods leaning up against the wall behind the bookcase.

The big television set he had purchased only last month; that was safe, too.

Everything, all he owned, was untouched. Safe. Unharmed.

'Dinner won't be ready for half an hour,' Laura murmured anxiously, unfastening her apron. 'I didn't expect you home so early. I've just been sitting around all day. I did clean the stove. Some salesman left a sample of a new cleanser.'

'That's OK.' He examined a favorite Renoir print on the wall. 'Take your time. It's good to see all these things again. I—'

From the bedroom a crying sound came. Laura turned quickly. 'I guess we woke up Jimmy.'

'Jimmy?'

Laura laughed. 'Darling, don't you remember your own son?'

'Of course,' Paine murmured, annoyed. He followed Laura slowly into the bedroom. 'Just for a minute everything seemed strange.' He rubbed his forehead, frowning. 'Strange and unfamiliar. Sort of out of focus.'

They stood by the crib, gazing down at the baby. Jimmy glared back up at his mother and dad.

'It must have been the sun,' Laura said. 'It's so terribly hot outside.'

'That must be it. I'm OK now.' Paine reached down and poked at the baby. He put his arm around his wife, hugging her to him. 'It must have been the sun,' he said. He looked down into her eyes and smiled.

Introduction by David Farr

Story & Script Title: The Impossible Planet

David Farr is a theatre and film writer and director known for the television series The Night Manager, for which he wrote the screenplay, and the feature film The Ones Below, which he wrote and directed. Farr also wrote the screenplay for the 2011 feature film Hanna, which he is currently developing into a television series.

The Impossible Planet is a very short story. It runs to just a few pages and is really just one simple idea. But when I read it I just fell in love with the proposition – two galactic nobodies think they can make a mint out of a VERY old lady by taking her on a ride on a spaceship to nowhere. But who is kidding who?

It's one of Philip K Dick's great gifts that even his simplest stories conjure timeless themes. *The Impossible Planet* deals with loss, the past, memory, and our terror that life on Earth is ephemeral and possibly doomed. It questions what it is to be human, and has a robot who may be more emotionally loyal than either of its mortal protagonists. In doing so it questions what it is to have a soul.

At heart the story is a moral tale. When I adapted it I added a strangely romantic element that isn't really in the story but just leapt out at me. That's the pleasure of adaptation.

It's like digging in the original for what is inherent but not always expressed. In this case lost love, lost paradise, and the possibility of it being regained.

For such a slight story, *The Impossible Planet* is suffused with a strange loss and nostalgia for many things, and most of all for an earth that no longer exists.

Or does it?

THE IMPOSSIBLE PLANET

'She just stands there,' Norton said nervously, 'Captain, you'll have to talk to her.'

'What does she want?'

'She wants a ticket. She's stone deaf. She just stands there staring and she won't go away. It gives me the creeps.'

Captain Andrews got slowly to his feet. 'Okay. I'll talk to her. Send her in.'

'Thanks.' To the corridor Norton said, 'The Captain will talk to you. Come ahead.'

There was motion outside the control room. A flash of metal. Captain Andrews pushed his desk scanner back and stood waiting.

'In here.' Norton backed into the control room. 'This way. Right in here.'

Behind Norton came a withered little old woman. Beside her moved a gleaming robant, a towering robot servant, supporting her with its arm. The robant and the tiny old woman entered the control room slowly.

'Here's her papers.' Norton slid a folio onto the chart desk, his voice awed. 'She's three hundred and fifty years old. One of the oldest sustained. From Riga II.'

Andrews leafed slowly through the folio. In front of the desk the little woman stood silently, staring straight ahead. Her faded eyes were pale blue. Like ancient china.

'Irma Vincent Gordon,' Andrews murmured. He glanced up. 'Is that right?'

The old woman did not answer.

'She is totally deaf, sir,' the robant said.

Andrews grunted and returned to the folio. Irma Gordon was one of the original settlers of the Riga system. Origin unknown. Probably born out in space in one of the old sub-C ships. A strange feeling drifted through him. The little old creature. The centuries she had seen! The changes.

'She wants to travel?' he asked the robant.

'Yes, sir. She has come from her home to purchase a ticket.'

'Can she stand space travel?'

'She came from Riga, here to Fomalhaut IX.'

'Where does she want to go?'

'To Earth, sir,' the robant said.

'*Earth!*' Andrews' jaw dropped. He swore nervously. 'What do you mean?'

'She wishes to travel to Earth, sir.'

'You see?' Norton muttered. 'Completely crazy.'

Gripping his desk tightly, Andrews addressed the old woman. 'Madam, we can't sell you a ticket to Earth.'

'She can't hear you, sir,' the robant said.

Andrews found a piece of paper. He wrote in big letters:

CAN'T SELL YOU A TICKET TO EARTH

He held it up. The old woman's eyes moved as she studied the words. Her lips twitched. 'Why not?' she said at last. Her voice was faint and dry. Like rustling weeds.

Andrews scratched an answer.

NO SUCH PLACE

He added grimly:

MYTH—LEGEND—NEVER EXISTED

The old woman's faded eyes left the words. She gazed directly at Andrews, her face expressionless. Andrews became uneasy. Beside him, Norton sweated nervously.

'Jeez,' Norton muttered. 'Get her out of here. She'll put the hex on us.'

Andrews addressed the robant. 'Can't you make her understand. There is no such place as Earth. It's been proved a thousand times. No such primordial planet existed. All scientists agree human life arose simultaneously throughout the—'

'It is her wish to travel to Earth,' the robant said patiently. 'She is three hundred and fifty years old and they have ceased giving her sustentation treatments. She wishes to visit Earth before she dies.'

'But it's a myth!' Andrews exploded. He opened and closed his mouth, but no words came.

'How much?' the old woman said. 'How much?'

'I can't do it!' Andrews shouted. 'There isn't—'

'We have a kilo positives,' the robant said.

Andrews became suddenly quiet. 'A thousand positives.' He blanched in amazement. His jaws clamped shut, the color draining from his face.

'How much?' the old woman repeated. 'How much?'

'Will that be sufficient?' the robant asked.

For a moment Andrews swallowed silently. Abruptly he found his voice. 'Sure,' he said. 'Why not?'

'Captain!' Norton protested. 'Have you gone nuts? You know there's no such place as Earth! How the hell can we—'

'Sure, we'll take her.' Andrews buttoned his tunic slowly, hands shaking. 'We'll take her anywhere she wants to go. Tell her that. For a thousand positives we'll be glad to take her to Earth. Okay?'

'Of course,' the robant said. 'She has saved many decades for this. She will give you the kilo positives at once. She has them with her.'

'Look,' Norton said. 'You can get twenty years for this. They'll take your articles and your card and they'll—'

'Shut up.' Andrews spun the dial of the intersystem vidsender. Under them the jets throbbed and roared. The lumbering transport had reached deep space. 'I want the main information library at Centaurus II,' he said into the speaker.

'Even for a thousand positives you can't do it. Nobody can do it. They tried to find Earth for generations. Directorate ships tracked down every moth-eaten planet in the whole—'

The vidsender clicked. 'Centaurus II.'

'Information library.'

Norton caught Andrews' arm. 'Please, Captain. Even for *two* kilo positives—'

'I want the following information,' Andrews said into the vidspeaker. 'All facts that are known concerning the planet Earth. Legendary birthplace of the human race.'

'No facts are known,' the detached voice of the library monitor came. 'The subject is classified as metaparticular.'

'What unverified but widely circulated reports have survived?'

'Most legends concerning Earth were lost during the Centauran-Rigan conflict of 4-B33a. What survived is fragmentary. Earth is variously described as a large ringed planet with three moons, as a small, dense planet with a single moon, as the first planet of a ten-planet system located around a dwarf white—'

'What's the most prevalent legend?'

'The Morrison Report of 5-C2 1r analyzed the total ethnic and subliminal accounts of the legendary Earth. The final summation noted that Earth is generally considered to be a small third planet of a nine-planet system, with a single moon. Other than that, no agreement of legends could be constructed.'

'I see. A third planet of a nine-planet system. With a single moon.' Andrews broke the circuit and the screen faded.

'So?' Norton said.

Andrews got quickly to his feet. 'She probably knows every legend about it.' He pointed down—at the passenger quarters below. 'I want to get the accounts straight.'

'Why? What are you going to do?'

Andrews flipped open the master star chart. He ran his fingers down the index and released the scanner. In a moment it turned up a card.

He grabbed the chart and fed it into the robant pilot. 'The Emphor System,' he murmured thoughtfully.

'Emphor? We're going there?'

'According to the chart, there are ninety systems that show a third planet of nine with a single moon. Of the ninety, Emphor is the closest. We're heading there now.'

'I don't get it,' Norton protested. 'Emphor is a routine trading system. Emphor III isn't even a Class D check point.'

Captain Andrews grinned tightly. 'Emphor III has a single moon, and it's the third of nine planets. That's all we want. Does anybody know any more about Earth?' He glanced downwards. 'Does *she* know any more about Earth?'

'I see,' Norton said slowly. 'I'm beginning to get the picture.'

Emphor III turned silently below them. A dull red globe, suspended among sickly clouds, its baked and corroded surface lapped by the congealed remains of ancient seas. Cracked, eroded cliffs jutted starkly up. The flat plains had been dug and stripped bare. Great gouged pits pocketed the surface, endless gaping sores.

Norton's face twisted in revulsion. 'Look at it. Is anything alive down there?'

Captain Andrews frowned. 'I didn't realize it was so gutted.' He crossed abruptly to the robant pilot. 'There's supposed to be an auto-grapple some place down there. I'll try to pick it up.'

'A grapple? You mean that waste is inhabited?'

'A few Emphorites. Degenerate trading colony of some sort.' Andrews consulted the card. 'Commercial ships come here occasionally. Contact with this region has been vague since the Centauran-Rigan War.'

The passage rang with a sudden sound. The gleaming robant and Mrs Gordon emerged through the doorway into the control room. The old woman's face was alive with excitement. 'Captain! Is that—is that Earth down there?'

Andrews nodded. 'Yes.'

The robant led Mrs Gordon over to the big viewscreen. The old woman's face twitched, ripples of emotion stirring her withered features. 'I can hardly believe that's really Earth. It seems impossible.'

Norton glanced sharply at Captain Andrews.

'It's Earth,' Andrews stated, not meeting Norton's glance. 'The moon should be around soon.'

The old woman did not speak. She had turned her back.

Andrews contacted the auto-grapple and hooked the robant pilot on. The transport shuddered and then began to drop, as the beam from Emphor caught it and took over.

'We're landing,' Andrews said to the old woman, touching her on the shoulder.

'She can't hear you, sir,' the robant said.

Andrews grunted. 'Well, she can see.'

Below them the pitted, ruined surface of Emphor III was rising rapidly. The ship entered the cloud belt and emerged, coasting over a barren plain that stretched as far as the eye could see.

'What happened down there?' Norton said to Andrews. 'The war?'

'War. Mining. And it's old. The pits are probably bomb craters. Some of the long trenches may be scoop gouges. Looks like they really exhausted this place.'

A crooked row of broken mountain peaks shot past under them. They were nearing the remain of an ocean. Dark, unhealthy water lapped below, a vast sea, crusted with salt and waste, its edges disappearing into banks of piled debris.

'Why is it that way?' Mrs Gordon said suddenly. Doubt crossed her features. 'Why?'

'What do you mean?' Andrews said.

'I don't understand.' She stared uncertainly down at the surface below.

'It isn't supposed to be this way. Earth is green. Green and alive. Blue water and . . .' Her voice trailed off uneasily. '*Why?*'

Andrews grabbed some paper and wrote:

COMMERCIAL OPERATIONS EXHAUSTED SURFACE

Mrs Gordon studied his words, her lips twitching. A spasm moved through her, shaking the thin, dried-out body. 'Exhausted . . .' Her voice rose in shrill dismay. 'It's not supposed to be this way! I don't *want* it this way!'

The robant took her arm. 'She had better rest. I'll return her to her quarters. Please notify us when the landing has been made.'

'Sure.' Andrews nodded awkwardly as the robant led the old woman from the viewscreen. She clung to the guide rail, face distorted with fear and bewilderment.

'Something's wrong!' she wailed. 'Why is it this way? Why . . .'

The robant led her from the control room. The closing of the hydraulic safety doors cut off her thin cry abruptly.

Andrews relaxed, his body sagging. 'God.' He lit a cigarette shakily. 'What a racket she makes.'

'We're almost down,' Norton said frigidly.

Cold wind lashed at them as they stepped out cautiously. The air smelled bad—sour and acrid. Like rotten eggs. The wind brought salt and sand blowing up against their faces.

A few miles off the thick sea lay. They could hear it swishing faintly, gummily. A few birds passed silently overhead, great wings flapping soundlessly.

'Depressing damn place,' Andrews muttered.

'Yeah. I wonder what the old lady's thinking.'

Down the descent ramp came the glittering robant, helping the little old woman. She moved hesitantly, unsteady, gripping the robant's metal arm. The cold wind whipped around her frail body. For a moment she tottered—and then came on, leaving the ramp and gaining the uneven ground.

Norton shook his head. 'She looks bad. This air. And the wind.'

'I know.' Andrews moved back towards Mrs Gordon and the robant. 'How is she?' he asked.

'She is not well, sir,' the robant answered.

'Captain,' the old woman whispered.

'What is it?'

'You must tell me the truth. Is this—is this really Earth?' She watched his lips closely. 'You swear it is? You *swear*?' Her voice rose in shrill terror.

'It's Earth!' Andrews snapped irritably. 'I told you before. Of course it's Earth.'

'It doesn't look like Earth.' Mrs Gordon clung to his answer, panic-stricken. 'It doesn't look like Earth, Captain. Is it really Earth?'

'Yes!'

Her gaze wandered towards the ocean. A strange look flickered across her tired face, igniting her faded eyes with sudden hunger. 'Is that water? I want to see.'

Andrews turned to Norton. 'Get the launch out. Drive her where she wants.'

Norton pulled back angrily. 'Me?'

'That's an order.'

'Okay.' Norton returned reluctantly to the ship. Andrews lit a cigarette moodily and waited. Presently the launch slid out of the ship, coasting across the ash towards them.

'You can show her anything she wants,' Andrews said to the robant. 'Norton will drive you.'

'Thank you, sir,' the robant said. 'She will be grateful. She has wanted all her life to stand on Earth. She remembers her grandfather telling her about it. She believes that he came from Earth, a long time ago. She is very old. She is the last living member of her family.'

'But Earth is just a—' Andrews caught him. 'I mean—'

'Yes, sir. But she is very old. And she has waited many years.' The robant turned to the old woman and led her gently toward the launch. Andrews stared after them sullenly, rubbing his jaw and frowning.

'Okay,' Norton's voice came from the launch. He slid the hatch open and the robant led the old woman carefully inside. The hatch closed after them.

A moment later the launch shot away across the salt flat, towards the ugly, lapping ocean.

Norton and Captain Andrews paced restlessly along the shore. The sky was darkening. Sheets of salt blew against them. The mud flats stank in the gathering gloom of night. Dimly, off in the distance, a line of hills faded into the silence and vapors.

'Go on,' Andrews said, 'What then?'

'That's all. She got out of the launch. She and the robant. I stayed inside. They stood looking across the ocean. After a while the old woman sent the robant back to the launch.'

'Why?'

'I don't know. She wanted to be alone, I suppose. She stood for a time by herself. On the shore. Looking over the water. The wind rising. All at once she just sort of settled down. She sank down in a heap, into the salt ash.'

'Then what?'

'While I was pulling myself together, the robant leaped out and ran to her. It picked her up. It stood for a second and then it started for the water. I leaped out of the launch, yelling. It stepped into the water and disappeared. Sank down in the mud and filth. Vanished.' Norton shuddered. 'With her body.'

Andrews tossed his cigarette savagely away. The cigarette rolled off, glowing behind them. 'Anything more?'

'Nothing. It all happened in a second. She was standing there, looking over the water. Suddenly she quivered—like a dead branch. Then she just sort of dwindled away. And the robant was out of the launch and into the water with her before I could figure out what was happening.'

The sky was almost dark. Huge clouds drifted across the faint stars. Clouds of unhealthy night vapors and particles of waste. A flock of immense birds crossed the horizon, flying silently.

Against the broken hills the moon was rising. A diseased, barren globe, tinted faintly yellow. Like old parchment.

'Let's get back in the ship,' Andrews said. 'I don't like this place.'

'I can't figure out why it happened. The old woman.' Norton shook his head.

'The wind. Radioactive toxins. I checked with Centaurus II. The War devastated the whole system. Left the planet a lethal wreck.'

'Then we won't—'

'No. We won't have to answer for it.' They continued for a time in silence. 'We won't have to explain. It's evident enough. Anybody coming here, especially an old person—'

'Only nobody would come here,' Norton said bitterly. 'Especially an old person.'

Andrews didn't answer. He paced along, head down, hands in pockets. Norton followed silently behind. Above them, the single moon grew brighter as it escaped the mists and entered a patch of clear sky.

'By the way,' Norton said, his voice cold and distant behind Andrews. 'This is the last trip I'll be making with you. While I was in the ship I filed a formal request for new papers.'

'Oh.'

'Thought I'd let you know. And my share of the kilo positives. You can keep it.'

Andrews flushed and increased his pace, leaving Norton behind. The old woman's death had shaken him. He lit another cigarette and then threw it away.

Damn it—the fault wasn't *his*. She had been old. Three hundred and fifty years. Senile and deaf. A faded leaf, carried off by the wind. By the poisonous wind that lashed and twisted endlessly across the ruined face of the planet.

The ruined face. Salt ash and debris. The broken line of crumbling hills. And the silence. The eternal silence. Nothing but the wind and the lapping of the thick stagnant water. And the dark birds overhead.

Something glinted. Something at his feet, in the salt ash. Reflecting the sickly pallor of the moon.

Andrews bent down and groped in the darkness. His fingers closed over something hard. He picked the small disc up and examined it.

'Strange,' he said.

It wasn't until they were out in deep space, roaring back towards Fomalhaut, that he remembered the disc.

He slid away from the control panel, searching his pockets for it.

The disc was worn and thin. And terribly old. Andrews rubbed it and spat on it until it was clean enough to make out. A faint impression—nothing more. He turned it over. A token? Washer? Coin?

On the back were a few meaningless letters. Some ancient, forgotten script. He held the disc to the light until he made the letters out.

E PLURIBUS UNUM

He shrugged, tossed the ancient bit of metal into a waste disposal unit beside him, and turned his attention to the star charts, and home . . .

Introduction by Dee Rees

Story Title: The Hanging Stranger
Script Title: Kill All Others

Dee Rees is an American screenwriter and director known for her feature films Pariah, Bessie, and Mudbound, which was picked up from the Sundance Film Festival by Netflix in 2017.

'Going home – with their minds dead.'

This is the line that rings out from the bent narrative of *The Hanging Stranger* and this is the brilliant, singular line that hooked me into taking on this story. Ed Loyce leads us through a nightmarish world of collective unconsciousness; he is the last 'rational' man in an irrational world and there is such delicious perversity in the fact that he is the one who is made to feel crazy. In this story, the horrors happen in the daylight and the monsters hide in plain sight. In this story, the spectre is literal and physical – a hanging body from the square. But in principal, Philip K. Dick illustrates that in real life, the spectre can be much darker, much more insidious. It could be words, it could be an attitude, it could be an idea. And obliviousness is the real alien that destroys . . . 'Going home – with their minds dead.'

As Ed Loyce increasingly questions his judgment, we as readers also start questioning his reliability as a witness. Is he really seeing what he's seeing? Is he overreacting to something that's easily explained? Maybe things aren't as bad as they seem after all. Paranoia bends the story and Ed backward on himself and by the end we are a little bit more aware of what we don't see.

In a society where we rely upon pundits, analysts, and various forms of social media to shape our responses and tell us what we should feel and think, the twin viruses of complacency and apathy are given entre into our psyche. Numbing us out. The 'alien forces' that come to invade our minds are our own creation.

I adapted this story into the screenplay for *Kill All Others* during the throes of the 2016 US presidential campaign. There was blind, chanting jingoism. Many dangerous ideas were declared, nurtured, and allowed to propagate. There were many debates about 'literalism' vs. hyperbole; there were many debates about freedom of speech; there were many debates about nationalism. This is not really happening, they said. What you are seeing is not what you are really seeing, they said. What you are hearing is not really what is meant, they said. There were many debates about the wrong thing altogether. We didn't see it.

There was a body hanging in the square.

THE HANGING STRANGER

At five o'clock Ed Loyce washed up, tossed on his hat and coat, got his car out and headed across town toward his TV sales store. He was tired. His back and shoulders ached from digging dirt out of the basement and wheeling it into the back yard. But for a forty-year-old man he had done okay. Janet could get a new vase with the money he had saved; and he liked the idea of repairing the foundations himself.

It was getting dark. The setting sun cast long rays over the scurrying commuters, tired and grim-faced, women loaded down with bundles and packages, students, swarming home from the university, mixing with clerks and businessmen and drab secretaries. He stopped his Packard for a red light and then started it up again. The store had been opened without him; he'd arrive just in time to spell the help for dinner, go over the records of the day, maybe even close a couple of sales himself. He drove slowly past the small square of green in the center of the street, the town park. There were no parking places in front of LOYCE TV SALES AND SERVICE. He cursed under his breath and swung the car in a U-turn. Again he passed the little square of green with its lonely drinking fountain and bench and single lamppost.

From the lamppost something was hanging. A shapeless dark bundle, swinging a little with the wind. Like a dummy of some sort. Loyce rolled down his window and peered out. What the hell was it? A display of some kind? Sometimes the Chamber of Commerce put up displays in the square.

Again he made a U-turn and brought his car around. He passed the park and concentrated on the dark bundle. It wasn't a dummy. And if it was a display it was a strange kind. The hackles on his neck rose and he swallowed uneasily. Sweat slid out on his face and hands.

It was a body. A human body.

'Look at it!' Loyce snapped. 'Come on out here!'

Don Fergusson came slowly out of the store, buttoning his pinstripe coat with dignity. 'This is a big deal, Ed. I can't just leave the guy standing there.'

'See it?' Ed pointed into the gathering gloom. The lamp-post jutted up against the sky—the post and the bundle swinging from it. 'There it is. How the hell long has it been there?' His voice rose excitedly. 'What's wrong with everybody? They just walk on past!'

Don Fergusson lit a cigarette slowly. 'Take it easy, old man. There must be a good reason, or it wouldn't be there.'

'A reason! What kind of a reason?'

Fergusson shrugged. 'Like the time the Traffic Safety Council put that wrecked Buick there. Some sort of civic thing. How would I know?'

Jack Potter from the shoe shop joined them. 'What's up, boys?'

'There's a body hanging from the lamppost,' Loyce said. 'I'm going to call the cops.'

'They must know about it,' Potter said. 'Or otherwise it wouldn't be there.'

'I got to get back in.' Fergusson headed back into the store. 'Business before pleasure.'

Loyce began to get hysterical. 'You see it? You see it hanging there? A man's body! A dead man!'

'Sure, Ed. I saw it this afternoon when I went out for coffee.'

'You mean it's been there all afternoon?'

'Sure. What's the matter?' Potter glanced at his watch. 'Have to run. See you later, Ed.'

Potter hurried off, joining the flow of people moving along the sidewalk. Men and women, passing by the park. A few glanced up curiously at the dark bundle—and then went on. Nobody stopped. Nobody paid any attention.

'I'm going nuts,' Loyce whispered. He made his way to the curb and crossed out into traffic, among the cars. Horns honked angrily at him. He gained the curb and stepped up onto the little square of green.

The man had been middle-aged. His clothing was ripped and torn, a gray suit, splashed and caked with dried mud. A stranger. Loyce had never seen him before. Not a local man. His face was partly turned away, and in the evening wind he spun a little, turning gently, silently. His skin was gouged and cut. Red gashes, deep scratches of congealed blood. A pair of steel-rimmed glasses hung from one ear, dangling foolishly. His eyes bulged. His mouth was open, tongue thick and ugly blue.

'For Heaven's sake,' Loyce muttered, sickened. He pushed down his nausea and made his way back to the sidewalk. He was shaking all over, with revulsion—and fear.

Why? Who was the man? Why was he hanging there? What did it mean?

And—why didn't anybody notice?

He bumped into a small man hurrying along the sidewalk. 'Watch it!' the man grated. 'Oh, it's you, Ed.'

Ed nodded dazedly. 'Hello, Jenkins.'

'What's the matter?' The stationery clerk caught Ed's arm. 'You look sick.'

'The body. There in the park.'

'Sure, Ed.' Jenkins led him into the alcove of LOYCE TV SALES AND SERVICE. 'Take it easy.'

Margaret Henderson from the jewelry store joined them. 'Something wrong?'

'Ed's not feeling well.'

Loyce yanked himself free. 'How can you stand here? Don't you see it? For God's sake—'

'What's he talking about?' Margaret asked nervously.

'The body!' Ed shouted. 'The body hanging there!'

More people collected. 'Is he sick? It's Ed Loyce. You okay, Ed?'

'The body!' Loyce screamed, struggling to get past them. Hands caught at him. He tore loose. 'Let me go! The police! Get the police!'

'Ed—'

'Better get a doctor!'

'He must be sick.'

'Or drunk.'

Loyce fought his way through the people. He stumbled and half fell. Through a blur he saw rows of faces, curious, concerned, anxious. Men and women halting to see what the disturbance was. He fought past them toward his store. He could see Fergusson inside talking to a man, showing him an Emerson TV set. Pete Foley in the back at the service counter, setting up a new Philco. Loyce shouted at them frantically. His voice was lost in the roar of traffic and the murmuring around him.

'Do something!' he screamed. 'Don't stand there! Do something! Something's wrong! Something's happened! Things are going on!'

The crowd melted respectfully for the two heavy-set cops moving efficiently toward Loyce.

'Name?' the cop with the notebook murmured.

'Loyce.' He mopped his forehead wearily. 'Edward C. Loyce. Listen to me. Back there—'

'Address?' the cop demanded. The police car moved swiftly through traffic, shooting among the cars and buses. Loyce sagged against the seat, exhausted and confused. He took a deep shuddering breath.

'1368 Hurst Road.'

'That's here in Pikeville?'

'That's right.' Loyce pulled himself up with a violent effort. 'Listen to me. Back there. In the square. Hanging from the lamppost—'

'Where were you today?' the cop behind the wheel demanded.

'Where?' Loyce echoed.

'You weren't in your shop, were you?'

'No.' He shook his head. 'No, I was home. Down in the basement.'

'In the *basement?*'

'Digging. A new foundation. Getting out the dirt to pour a cement frame. Why? What has that to do with—'

'Was anybody else down there with you?'

'No. My wife was downtown. My kids were at school.' Loyce looked from one heavy-set cop to the other. Hope flickered across his face, wild hope. 'You mean because I was down there I missed—the explanation? I didn't get in on it? Like everybody else?'

After a pause the cop with the notebook said: 'That's right. You missed the explanation.'

'Then it's official? The body—it's *supposed* to be hanging there?'

'It's supposed to be hanging there. For everybody to see.'

Ed Loyce grinned weakly. 'Good Lord. I guess I sort of went off the deep end. I thought maybe something had happened. You know, something like the Ku Klux Klan. Some kind of violence. Communists or Fascists taking over.'

He wiped his face with his breast-pocket handkerchief, his hands shaking. 'I'm glad to know it's on the level.'

'It's on the level.' The police car was getting near the Hall of Justice. The sun had set. The streets were gloomy and dark. The lights had not yet come on.

'I feel better,' Loyce said. 'I was pretty excited there, for a minute. I guess I got all stirred up. Now that I understand, there's no need to take me in, is there?'

The two cops said nothing.

'I should be back at my store. The boys haven't had dinner. I'm all right, now. No more trouble. Is there any need of—'

'This won't take long,' the cop behind the wheel interrupted. 'A short process. Only a few minutes.'

'I hope it's short,' Loyce muttered. The car slowed down for a stoplight. 'I guess I sort of disturbed the peace. Funny, getting excited like that and—'

Loyce yanked the door open. He sprawled out into the street and rolled to his feet. Cars were moving all around him, gaining speed as the light changed. Loyce leaped onto the curb and raced among the people, burrowing into the swarming crowds. Behind him he heard sounds, shouts, people running.

They weren't cops. He had realized that right away. He knew every cop in Pikeville. A man couldn't own a store, operate a business in a small town for twenty-five years without getting to know all the cops.

They weren't cops—and there hadn't been any explanation. Potter, Fergusson, Jenkins, none of them knew why it was there. They didn't know—and they didn't care. *That* was the strange part.

Loyce ducked into a hardware store. He raced toward the back, past the startled clerks and customers, into the shipping room and through the back door. He tripped over a garbage can and ran up a flight of concrete steps. He climbed over a fence and jumped down on the other side, gasping and panting.

There was no sound behind him. He had got away.

He was at the entrance of an alley, dark and strewn with boards and ruined boxes and tires. He could see the street at the far end. A street light wavered and came on. Men and women. Stores. Neon signs. Cars.

And to his right—the police station.

He was close, terribly close. Past the loading platform of a grocery store rose the white concrete side of the Hall of Justice. Barred windows. The police antenna. A great concrete wall rising up in the darkness. A bad place for him to be near. He was too close. He had to keep moving, get farther away from them.

Them?

Loyce moved cautiously down the alley. Beyond the police station was the City Hall, the old-fashioned yellow structure of wood and gilded brass and broad cement steps. He could see the endless rows of offices, dark windows, the cedars and beds of flowers on each side of the entrance.

And—something else.

Above the City Hall was a patch of darkness, a cone of gloom denser than the surrounding night. A prism of black that spread out and was lost into the sky.

He listened. Good God, he could hear something. Something that made him struggle frantically to close his ears, his mind, to shut out the sound. A buzzing. A distant, muted hum like a great swarm of bees.

Loyce gazed up, rigid with horror. The splotch of darkness, hanging over the City Hall. Darkness so thick it seemed almost solid. *In the vortex something moved.* Flickering shapes. Things, descending from the sky, pausing momentarily above

the City Hall, fluttering over it in a dense swarm and then
dropping silently onto the roof.

Shapes. Fluttering shapes from the sky. From the crack of
darkness that hung above him.

He was seeing—them.

For a long time Loyce watched, crouched behind a sagging
fence in a pool of scummy water.

They were landing. Coming down in groups, landing
on the roof of the City Hall and disappearing inside. They
had wings. Like giant insects of some kind. They flew and
fluttered and came to rest—and then crawled crab-fashion,
sideways, across the roof and into the building.

He was sickened. And fascinated. Cold night wind blew
around him and he shuddered. He was tired, dazed with
shock. On the front steps of the City Hall were men, standing
here and there. Groups of men coming out of the building
and halting for a moment before going on.

Were there more of them?

It didn't seem possible. What he saw descending from
the black chasm weren't men. They were alien—from some
other world, some other dimension. Sliding through this slit,
this break in the shell of the universe. Entering through this
gap, winged insects from another realm of being.

On the steps of the City Hall a group of men broke up.
A few moved toward a waiting car. One of the remaining
shapes started to re-enter the City Hall. It changed its mind
and turned to follow the others.

Loyce closed his eyes in horror. His senses reeled. He
hung on tight, clutching at the sagging fence. The shape, the
man-shape, had abruptly fluttered up and flapped after the
others. It flew to the sidewalk and came to rest among them.

Pseudo-men. Imitation men. Insects with ability to disguise

themselves as men. Like other insects familiar to Earth. Protective coloration. Mimicry.

Loyce pulled himself away. He got slowly to his feet. It was night. The alley was totally dark. But maybe they could see in the dark. Maybe darkness made no difference to them.

He left the alley cautiously and moved out onto the street. Men and women flowed past, but not so many, now. At the bus stops stood waiting groups. A huge bus lumbered along the street, its lights flashing in the evening gloom.

Loyce moved forward. He pushed his way among those waiting and when the bus halted he boarded it and took a seat in the rear, by the door. A moment later the bus moved into life and rumbled down the street.

Loyce relaxed a little. He studied the people around him. Dulled, tired faces. People going home from work. Quite ordinary faces. None of them paid any attention to him. All sat quietly, sunk down in their seats, jiggling with the motion of the bus.

The man sitting next to him unfolded a newspaper. He began to read the sports section, his lips moving. An ordinary man. Blue suit. Tie. A businessman, or a salesman. On his way home to his wife and family.

Across the aisle a young woman, perhaps twenty. Dark eyes and hair, a package on her lap. Nylons and heels. Red coat and white Angora sweater. Gazing absently ahead of her.

A high school boy in jeans and black jacket.

A great triple-chinned woman with an immense shopping bag loaded with packages and parcels. Her thick face dim with weariness.

Ordinary people. The kind that rode the bus every evening. Going home to their families. To dinner.

Going home—with their minds dead. Controlled, filmed over with the mask of an alien being that had appeared and taken possession of them, their town, their lives. Himself, too. Except that he happened to be deep in his cellar instead of in the store. Somehow, he had been overlooked. They had missed him. Their control wasn't perfect, foolproof.

Maybe there were others.

Hope flickered in Loyce. They weren't omnipotent. They had made a mistake, not got control of him. Their net, their field of control, had passed over him. He had emerged from his cellar as he had gone down. Apparently their power-zone was limited.

A few seats down the aisle a man was watching him. Loyce broke off his chain of thought. A slender man, with dark hair and a small mustache. Well-dressed, brown suit and shiny shoes. A book between his small hands. He was watching Loyce, studying him intently. He turned quickly away.

Loyce tensed. One of *them*? Or—another they had missed?

The man was watching him again. Small dark eyes, alive and clever. Shrewd. A man too shrewd for them—or one of the things itself, an alien insect from beyond.

The bus halted. An elderly man got on slowly and dropped his token into the box. He moved down the aisle and took a seat opposite Loyce.

The elderly man caught the sharp-eyed man's gaze. For a split second something passed between them.

A look rich with meaning.

Loyce got to his feet. The bus was moving. He ran to the door. One step down into the well. He yanked the emergency door release. The rubber door swung open.

'Hey!' the driver shouted, jamming on the brakes. 'What the hell—?'

Loyce squirmed through. The bus was slowing down. Houses on all sides. A residential district, lawns and tall apartment buildings. Behind him, the bright-eyed man had leaped up. The elderly man was also on his feet. They were coming after him.

Loyce leaped. He hit the pavement with terrific force and rolled against the curb. Pain lapped over him. Pain and a vast tide of blackness. Desperately, he fought it off. He struggled to his knees and then slid down again. The bus had stopped. People were getting off.

Loyce groped around. His fingers closed over something. A rock, lying in the gutter. He crawled to his feet, grunting with pain. A shape loomed before him. A man, the bright-eyed man with the book.

Loyce kicked. The man gasped and fell. Loyce brought the rock down. The man screamed and tried to roll away. '*Stop!* For God's sake listen—'

He struck again. A hideous crunching sound. The man's voice cut off and dissolved in a bubbling wail. Loyce scrambled up and back. The others were there, now. All around him. He ran, awkwardly, down the sidewalk, up a driveway. None of them followed him. They had stopped and were bending over the inert body of the man with the book, the bright-eyed man who had come after him.

Had he made a mistake?

But it was too late to worry about that. He had to get out—away from them. Out of Pikeville, beyond the crack of darkness, the rent between their world and his.

'Ed!' Janet Loyce backed away nervously. 'What is it? What—'

Ed Loyce slammed the door behind him and came into the living room. 'Pull down the shades. Quick.'

Janet moved toward the window. 'But—'

'Do as I say. Who else is here besides you?'

'Nobody. Just the twins. They're upstairs in their room. What's happened? You look so strange. Why are you home?'

Ed locked the front door. He prowled around the house, into the kitchen. From the drawer under the sink he slid out the big butcher knife and ran his finger along it. Sharp. Plenty sharp. He returned to the living room.

'Listen to me,' he said. 'I don't have much time. They know I escaped and they'll be looking for me.'

'Escaped?' Janet's face twisted with bewilderment and fear. 'Who?'

'The town has been taken over. They're in control. I've got it pretty well figured out. They started at the top, at the City Hall and police department. What they did with the *real* humans they—'

'What are you talking about?'

'We've been invaded. From some other universe, some other dimension. They're insects. Mimicry. And more. Power to control minds. Your mind.'

'My mind?'

'Their entrance is *here*, in Pikeville. They've taken over all of you. The whole town—except me. We're up against an incredibly powerful enemy, but they have their limitations. That's our hope. They're limited! They can make mistakes!'

Janet shook her head. 'I don't understand, Ed. You must be insane.'

'Insane? No. Just lucky. If I hadn't been down in the basement I'd be like all the rest of you.' Loyce peered out the window. 'But I can't stand here talking. Get your coat.'

'My coat?'

'We're getting out of here. Out of Pikeville. We've got to get help. Fight this thing. They *can* be beaten. They're not infallible. It's going to be close—but we may make it if we hurry. Come on!' He grabbed her arm roughly. 'Get

your coat and call the twins. We're all leaving. Don't stop
to pack. There's no time for that.'

White-faced, his wife moved toward the closet and got
down her coat. 'Where are we going?'

Ed pulled open the desk drawer and spilled the contents
out onto the floor. He grabbed up a road map and spread
it open. 'They'll have the highway covered, of course. But
there's a back road. To Oak Grove. I got onto it once. It's
practically abandoned. Maybe they'll forget about it.'

'The old Ranch Road? Good Lord—it's completely closed.
Nobody's supposed to drive over it.'

'I know.' Ed thrust the map grimly into his coat. 'That's
our best chance. Now call down the twins and let's get
going. Your car is full of gas, isn't it?'

Janet was dazed.

'The Chevy? I had it filled up yesterday afternoon.' Janet
moved toward the stairs. 'Ed, I—'

'Call the twins!' Ed unlocked the front door and peered
out. Nothing stirred. No sign of life. All right so far.

'Come on downstairs,' Janet called in a wavering voice.
'We're—going out for a while.'

'Now?' Tommy's voice came.

'Hurry up,' Ed barked. 'Get down here, both of you.'

Tommy appeared at the top of the stairs. 'I was doing my
homework. We're starting fractions. Miss Parker says if we
don't get this done—'

'You can forget about fractions.' Ed grabbed his son as he
came down the stairs and propelled him toward the door.
'Where's Jim?'

'He's coming.'

Jim started slowly down the stairs. 'What's up, Dad?'

'We're going for a ride.'

'A ride? Where?'

Ed turned to Janet. 'We'll leave the lights on. And the TV set. Go turn it on.' He pushed her toward the set. 'So they'll think we're still—'

He heard the buzz. And dropped instantly, the long butcher knife out. Sickened, he saw it coming down the stairs at him, wings a blur of motion as it aimed itself. It still bore a vague resemblance to Jimmy. It was small, a baby one. A brief glimpse—the thing hurtling at him, cold, multi-lensed inhuman eyes. Wings, body still clothed in yellow T-shirt and jeans, the mimic outline still stamped on it. A strange half-turn of its body as it reached him. What was it doing?

A stinger.

Loyce stabbed wildly at it. It retreated, buzzing frantically. Loyce rolled and crawled toward the door. Tommy and Janet stood still as statues, faces blank. Watching without expression. Loyce stabbed again. This time the knife connected. The thing shrieked and faltered. It bounced against the wall and fluttered down.

Something lapped through his mind. A wall of force, energy, an alien mind probing into him. He was suddenly paralyzed. The mind entered his own, touched against him briefly, shockingly. An utter alien presence, settling over him—and then it flickered out as the thing collapsed in a broken heap on the rug.

It was dead. He turned it over with his foot. It was an insect, a fly of some kind. Yellow T-shirt, jeans. His son Jimmy . . . He closed his mind tight. It was too late to think about that. Savagely he scooped up his knife and headed toward the door. Janet and Tommy stood stone-still, neither of them moving.

The car was out. He'd never get through. They'd be waiting for him. It was ten miles on foot. Ten long miles over rough ground, gulleys and open fields and hills of uncut forest. He'd have to go alone.

Loyce opened the door. For a brief second he looked back at his wife and son. Then he slammed the door behind him and raced down the porch steps.

A moment later he was on his way, hurrying swiftly through the darkness toward the edge of town.

The early morning sunlight was blinding. Loyce halted, gasping for breath, swaying back and forth. Sweat ran down in his eyes. His clothing was torn, shredded by the brush and thorns through which he had crawled. Ten miles—on his hands and knees. Crawling, creeping through the night. His shoes were mud-caked. He was scratched and limping, utterly exhausted.

But ahead of him lay Oak Grove.

He took a deep breath and started down the hill. Twice he stumbled and fell, picking himself up and trudging on. His ears rang. Everything receded and wavered. But he was there. He had got out, away from Pikeville.

A farmer in a field gaped at him. From a house a young woman watched in wonder. Loyce reached the road and turned onto it. Ahead of him was a gasoline station and a drive-in. A couple of trucks, some chickens pecking in the dirt, a dog tied with a string.

The white-clad attendant watched suspiciously as he dragged himself up to the station. 'Thank God.' He caught hold of the wall. 'I didn't think I was going to make it. They followed me most of the way. I could hear them buzzing. Buzzing and flitting around behind me.'

'What happened?' the attendant demanded. 'You in a wreck? A hold-up?'

Loyce shook his head wearily. 'They have the whole town. The City Hall and the police station. They hung a man from the lamppost. That was the first thing I saw. They've got all the roads blocked. I saw them hovering over the cars coming in. About four this morning I got beyond them. I knew it right away. I could feel them leave. And then the sun came up.'

The attendant licked his lip nervously. 'You're out of your head. I better get a doctor.'

'Get me into Oak Grove,' Loyce gasped. He sank down on the gravel. 'We've got to get started—cleaning them out. Got to get started right away.'

They kept a tape recorder going all the time he talked. When he had finished the Commissioner snapped off the recorder and got to his feet. He stood for a moment, deep in thought. Finally he got out his cigarettes and lit up slowly, a frown on his beefy face.

'You don't believe me,' Loyce said.

The Commissioner offered him a cigarette. Loyce pushed it impatiently away. 'Suit yourself.' The Commissioner moved over to the window and stood for a time looking out at the town of Oak Grove. 'I believe you,' he said abruptly.

Loyce sagged. 'Thank God.'

'So you got away.' The Commissioner shook his head. 'You were down in your cellar instead of at work. A freak chance. One in a million.'

Loyce sipped some of the black coffee they had brought him. 'I have a theory,' he murmured.

'What is it?'

'About them. Who they are. They take over one area at a time. Starting at the top—the highest level of authority. Working down from there in a widening circle. When they're firmly in control they go on to the next town. They spread, slowly, very gradually. I think it's been going on for a long time.'

'A long time?'

'Thousands of years. I don't think it's new.'

'Why do you say that?'

'When I was a kid . . . A picture they showed us in Bible League. A religious picture—an old print. The enemy gods, defeated by Jehovah. Moloch, Beelzebub, Moab, Baalin, Ashtaroth—'

'So?'

'They were all represented by figures.' Loyce looked up at the Commissioner. 'Beelzebub was represented as—a giant fly.'

The Commissioner grunted. 'An old struggle.'

'They've been defeated. The Bible is an account of their defeats. They make gains—but finally they're defeated.'

'Why defeated?'

'They can't get everyone. They didn't get me. And they never got the Hebrews. The Hebrews carried the message to the whole world. The realization of the danger. The two men on the bus. I think they understood. Had escaped, like I did.' He clenched his fists. 'I killed one of them. I made a mistake. I was afraid to take a chance.'

The Commissioner nodded. 'Yes, they undoubtedly had escaped, as you did. Freak accidents. But the rest of the town was firmly in control.' He turned from the window, 'Well, Mr Loyce. You seem to have figured everything out.'

'Not everything. The hanging man. The dead man hanging from the lamppost. I don't understand that. *Why?* Why did they deliberately hang him there?'

'That would seem simple.' The Commissioner smiled faintly. '*Bait.*'

Loyce stiffened. His heart stopped beating. 'Bait? What do you mean?'

'To draw you out. Make you declare yourself. So they'd know who was under control—and who had escaped.'

Loyce recoiled with horror. 'Then they *expected* failures! They anticipated—' He broke off. 'They were ready with a trap.'

'And you showed yourself. You reacted. You made yourself known.' The Commissioner abruptly moved toward the door. 'Come along, Loyce. There's a lot to do. We must get moving. There's no time to waste.'

Loyce started slowly to his feet, numbed. 'And the man. *Who was the man?* I never saw him before. He wasn't a local man. He was a stranger. All muddy and dirty, his face cut, slashed—'

There was a strange look on the Commissioner's face as he answered, 'Maybe,' he said softly, 'you'll understand that, too. Come along with me, Mr Loyce.' He held the door open, his eyes gleaming. Loyce caught a glimpse of the street in front of the police station. Policemen, a platform of some sort. A telephone pole—and a rope! 'Right this way,' the Commissioner said, smiling coldly

As the sun set, the vice-president of the Oak Grove Merchants' Bank came up out of the vault, threw the heavy time locks, put on his hat and coat, and hurried outside onto the sidewalk. Only a few people were there, hurrying home to dinner.

'Good night,' the guard said, locking the door after him.

'Good night,' Clarence Mason murmured. He started along the street toward his car. He was tired. He had been working all day down in the vault, examining the layout of the safety deposit boxes to see if there was room for another tier. He was glad to be finished.

At the corner he halted. The street lights had not yet come on. The street was dim. Everything was vague. He looked around—and froze.

From the telephone pole in front of the police station, something large and shapeless hung. It moved a little with the wind.

What the hell was it?

Mason approached it warily. He wanted to get home. He was tired and hungry. He thought of his wife, his kids, a hot meal on the dinner table. But there was something about the dark bundle, something ominous and ugly. The light was bad; he couldn't tell what it was. Yet it drew him on, made him move closer for a better look. The shapeless thing made him uneasy. He was frightened by it. Frightened—and fascinated.

And the strange part was that nobody else seemed to notice it.

Introduction by Tony Grisoni

Story Title: Sales Pitch
Script Title: Crazy Diamond

Tony Grisoni is a writer and director known for Fear and Loathing in Las Vegas, the Red Riding trilogy, Southcliffe and In This World. He is currently adapting China Mieville's novel The City and the City into a television series for the BBC.

Some years ago, when researching into the life of Philip K. Dick, I chanced upon a small green frog that sat motionless on the shower head. Every morning the frog was there in the same position. I worried in case he should jump and land on me – the thought of that damp amphibious body! – but he remained motionless. For three days. Then on the third day I studied his face closely and was just thinking how there was a certain resemblance to PKD when he moved for the first time, turned his green head and looked straight back at me. I decided it was time to go home.

Philip K. Dick wrote *Sales Pitch* for *Future Science Fiction* magazine in 1954. The short story describes the stagnating lives of Ed and Sally. Ed's tedious commute from Ganymede to Earth, plagued by intrusive advertising, is not light-years away from many commuters' experience in this 21st century of rampant consumerism and surveillance that has invaded the most private corners of our lives. Ed's dream of starting over on the new worlds of Proxima Centaurus remains just that – an escapist fantasy. Meanwhile Ed's wife, Sally, opens the door to a 'Fasrad' – a domestic robot which has the answer to every problem a homeowner might have. What begins as a humorous – if insistent – flirtation spirals into full-blown farce as the Fasrad aggressively attempts to sell itself. The interloping robot terrorises the human couple and, in an effort to exorcise the Fasrad, Ed takes it on a doomed journey towards Proxima.

The story is powerfully informed by the burgeoning consumerism of the 50s, but there was something touching about this couple crushed by market forces. Ed and Sally are trusting and stoical and hopeful, they don't ask for much, but what they get is drudgery and economic slavery. So when freely adapting for the screen I kept Ed and Sally as the central characters, developing them and their relationship in line with other couples I found in Philip K. Dick's writing. Ed remains a dreamer – though now a fantasy mariner of the Seven Seas – and Sally, though apparently conventional and fond of homespun philosophy, harbours her own dark desires of adventure. The suburban couple are prisoners to relentless exhortations to care for an environment they have little control over – decisions being made from somewhere far outside their orbit.

In my version of the tale – guided by Phildickian themes – the interloper becomes a noir femme fatale and Ed is compromised by his attraction to her. Of course, in the end the femme fatale surprises us all with her serpentine scheming, but so does Sally, and Ed too when he is freed of everything he believed he owned. So in many ways the story returns to the original concerns of consumerism. PKD voiced his worries about the tale in 1978: 'I really deplore the ending. So when you read the story, try to imagine it as it ought to have been written. The Fasrad says, "Sir, I am here to help you. The hell with my sales pitch. Let's be together forever."' And so I hope Phil would approve of our new ending where humans and quasi-humans are indeed married forever – or at least for a foreseeable future – and I need worry no longer about a small green frog leaping on me in the shower.

Tony Grisoni
Stoke Newington, London
17 May 2017

SALES PITCH

Commute ships roared on all sides, as Ed Morris made his way wearily home to Earth at the end of a long hard day at the office. The Ganymede-Terra lanes were choked with exhausted, grim-faced businessmen; Jupiter was in opposition to Earth and the trip was a good two hours. Every few million miles the great flow slowed to a grinding, agonized halt; signal-lights flashed as streams from Mars and Saturn fed into the main traffic-arteries.

'Lord,' Morris muttered. 'How tired can you *get?*' He locked the autopilot and momentarily turned from the control-board to light a much-needed cigarette. His hands shook. His head swam. It was past six; Sally would be fuming; dinner would be spoiled. The same old thing. Nerve-wracking driving, honking horns and irate drivers zooming past his little ship, furious gesturing, shouting, cursing . . .

And the ads. That was what really did it. He could have stood everything else—but the ads, the whole long way from Ganymede to Earth. And on Earth, the swarms of sales robots; it was too much. And they were everywhere.

He slowed to avoid a fifty-ship smash-up. Repair-ships were scurrying around trying to get the debris out of the lane. His audio-speaker wailed as police rockets hurried up. Expertly, Morris raised his ship, cut between two slow-moving commercial transports, zipped momentarily into the unused left lane, and then sped on, the wreck left behind. Horns honked furiously at him; he ignored them.

'Trans-Solar Products greets you!' an immense voice boomed in his ear. Morris groaned and hunched down in his seat. He was getting near Terra; the barrage was increasing. 'Is your tension-index pushed over the safety-margin by the ordinary frustrations of the day? Then you need an Id-Persona Unit. So small it can be worn behind the ear, close to the frontal lobe—'

Thank God, he was past it. The ad dimmed and receded behind, as his fast-moving ship hurtled forward. But another was right ahead.

'Drivers! Thousands of unnecessary deaths each year from inter-planet driving. Hypno-Motor Control from an expert source-point ensures your safety. Surrender your body and save your life!' The voice roared louder. 'Industrial experts say—'

Both audio ads, the easiest to ignore. But now a visual ad was forming; he winced, closed his eyes, but it did no good.

'Men!' an unctuous voice thundered on all sides of him. 'Banish internally-caused obnoxious odors *forever*. Removal by modern painless methods of the gastrointestinal tract and substitution system will relieve you of the most acute cause of social rejection.' The visual image locked; a vast nude girl, blonde hair disarranged, blue eyes half shut, lips parted, head tilted back in sleep-drugged ecstasy. The features ballooned as the lips approached his own. Abruptly the orgiastic expression on the girl's face vanished. Disgust and revulsion swept across, and then the image faded out.

'Does this happen to you?' the voice boomed. 'During erotic sex-play do you offend your love-partner by the presence of gastric processes which—'

The voice died, and he was past. His mind his own again, Morris kicked savagely at the throttle and sent the little ship leaping. The pressure, applied directly to the audio-visual regions of his brain, had faded below spark point. He groaned and shook his head to clear it. All around him the vague half-defined echoes of ads glittered and gibbered, like ghosts of distant video-stations. Ads waited on all sides; he steered a careful course, dexterity born of animal desperation, but not all could be avoided. Despair seized him. The outline of a new visual-audio ad was already coming into being.

'You, mister wage-earner!' it shouted into the eyes and ears, noses and throats, of a thousand weary commuters. 'Tired of the same old job? Wonder Circuits Inc. has perfected a marvelous long-range thought-wave scanner. Know what others are thinking and saying. Get the edge on fellow employees. Learn facts, figures about your employer's personal existence. Banish uncertainty!'

Morris' despair swept up wildly. He threw the throttle on full blast; the little ship bucked and rolled as it climbed from the traffic-lane into the dead zone beyond. A shrieking roar, as his fender whipped through the protective wall—and then the ad faded behind him.

He slowed down, trembling with misery and fatigue. Earth lay ahead. He'd be home, soon. Maybe he could get a good night's sleep. He shakily dropped the nose of the ship and prepared to hook onto the tractor beam of the Chicago commute field.

'The best metabolism adjuster on the market,' the sales-robot shrilled. 'Guaranteed to maintain a perfect endocrine-balance, or your money refunded in full.'

Morris pushed wearily past the salesrobot, up the sidewalk toward the residential-block that contained his living-unit. The robot followed a few steps, then forgot him and hurried after another grim-faced commuter.

'All the news while it's news,' a metallic voice dinned at him. 'Have a retinal vidscreen installed in your least-used

eye. Keep in touch with the world; don't wait for out-of-
date hourly summaries.'

'*Get out of the way*,' Morris muttered. The robot stepped
aside for him and he crossed the street with a pack of
hunched-over men and women.

Robot-salesmen were everywhere, gesturing, pleading,
shrilling. One started after him and he quickened his pace.
It scurried along, chanting its pitch and trying to attract
his attention, all the way up the hill to his living-unit.
It didn't give up until he stooped over, snatched up a
rock, and hurled it futilely. He scrambled in the house
and slammed the doorlock after him. The robot hesitated,
then turned and raced after a woman with an armload of
packages toiling up the hill. She tried vainly to elude it,
without success.

'Darling!' Sally cried. She hurried from the kitchen, drying
her hands on her plastic shorts, bright-eyed and excited. 'Oh,
you poor thing! You look so tired!'

Morris peeled off his hat and coat and kissed his wife
briefly on her bare shoulder. 'What's for dinner?'

Sally gave his hat and coat to the closet. 'We're having
Uranian wild pheasant; your favorite dish.'

Morris' mouth watered, and a tiny surge of energy crawled
back into his exhausted body. 'No kidding? What the hell's
the occasion?'

His wife's brown eyes moistened with compassion.
'Darling, it's your birthday; you're thirty-seven years old
today. Had you forgotten?'

'Yeah,' Morris grinned a little. 'I sure had.' He wandered
into the kitchen. The table was set; coffee was steaming in the
cups and there was butter and white bread, mashed potatoes
and green peas. 'My golly. A real occasion.'

Sally punched the stove controls and the container of smoking pheasant was slid onto the table and neatly sliced open. 'Go wash your hands and we're ready to eat. Hurry— before it gets cold.'

Morris presented his hands to the wash slot and then sat down gratefully at the table. Sally served the tender, fragrant pheasant, and the two of them began eating.

'Sally,' Morris said, when his plate was empty and he was leaning back and sipping slowly at his coffee. 'I can't go on like this. Something's got to be done.'

'You mean the drive? I wish you could get a position on Mars like Bob Young. Maybe if you talked to the Employment Commission and explained to them how all the strain—'

'It's not just the drive. *They're right out front.* Everywhere. Waiting for me. All day and night.'

'Who are, dear?'

'Robots selling things. As soon as I set down the ship. Robots and visual-audio ads. They dig right into a man's brain. They follow people around until they die.'

'I know.' Sally patted his hand sympathetically. 'When I go shopping they follow me in clusters. All talking at once. It's really a panic—you can't understand half what they're saying.'

'We've got to break out.'

'Break out?' Sally faltered. 'What do you mean?'

'We've got to get away from them. They're destroying us.'

Morris fumbled in his pocket and carefully got out a tiny fragment of metal-foil. He unrolled it with painstaking care and smoothed it out on the table. 'Look at this. It was circulated in the office, among the men; it got to me and I kept it.'

'What does it mean?' Sally's brow wrinkled as she made out the words. 'Dear, I don't think you got all of it. There must be more than this.'

'A new world,' Morris said softly. 'Where they haven't got to, yet. It's a long way off, out beyond the solar system. Out in the stars.'

'Proxima?'

'Twenty planets. Half of them habitable. Only a few thousand people out there. Families, workmen, scientists, some industrial survey teams. Land free for the asking.'

'But it's so—' Sally made a face. 'Dear, isn't it sort of underdeveloped? They say it's like living back in the twentieth century. Flush toilets, bathtubs, gasoline driven cars—'

'That's right.' Morris rolled up the bit of crumpled metal, his face grim and dead-serious. 'It's a hundred years behind times. None of this.' He indicated the stove and the furnishings in the living room. 'We'll have to do without. We'll have to get used to a simpler life. The way our ancestors lived.' He tried to smile but his face wouldn't cooperate. 'You think you'd like it? No ads, no salesrobots, traffic moving at sixty miles an hour instead of sixty million. We could raise passage on one of the big trans-system liners. I could sell my commute rocket . . .'

There was a hesitant, doubtful silence.

'Ed,' Sally began. 'I think we should think it over more. What about your job? What would you do out there?'

'I'd find something.'

'But *what*? Haven't you got that part figured out?' A shrill tinge of annoyance crept into her voice. 'It seems to me we should consider that part just a little more before we throw away everything and just—take off.'

'If we don't go,' Morris said slowly, trying to keep his voice steady, 'they'll get us. There isn't much time left. I don't know how much longer I can hold them off.'

'Really, Ed! You make it sound so melodramatic. If you feel that bad why don't you take some time off and have a complete inhibition check? I was watching a vidprogram and I saw them going over a man whose psychosomatic system was much worse than yours. A much older man.'

She leaped to her feet. 'Let's go out tonight and celebrate. Okay?' Her slim fingers fumbled at the zipper of her shorts. 'I'll put on my new plastirobe, the one I've never had nerve enough to wear.'

Her eyes sparkled with excitement as she hurried into the bedroom. 'You know the one I mean? When you're up close it's translucent but as you get farther off it becomes more and more sheer until—'

'I know the one,' Morris said wearily. 'I've seen them advertised on my way home from work.' He got slowly to his feet and wandered into the living room. At the door of the bedroom he halted. 'Sally—'

'Yes?'

Morris opened his mouth to speak. He was going to ask her again, talk to her about the metal-foil fragment he had carefully wadded up and carried home. He was going to talk to her about the frontier. About Proxima Centauri. Going away and never coming back. But he never had a chance.

The doorchimes sounded.

'Somebody's at the door!' Sally cried excitedly. 'Hurry up and see who it is!'

In the evening darkness the robot was a silent, unmoving figure. A cold wind blew around it and into the house. Morris shivered and moved back from the door. 'What do you want?' he demanded. A strange fear licked at him. 'What is it?'

The robot was larger than any he had seen. Tall and broad, with heavy metallic grippers and elongated eye-lenses. Its upper trunk was a square tank instead of the usual cone.

It rested on four treads, not the customary two. It towered over Morris, almost seven feet high. Massive and solid.

'Good evening,' it said calmly. Its voice was whipped around by the night wind; it mixed with the dismal noises of evening, the echoes of traffic and the clang of distant street signals. A few vague shapes hurried through the gloom. The world was black and hostile.

'Evening,' Morris responded automatically. He found himself trembling. 'What are you selling?'

'I would like to show you a fasrad,' the robot said.

Morris' mind was numb; it refused to respond. What was a *fasrad*? There was something dreamlike and nightmarish going on. He struggled to get his mind and body together. 'A what?' he croaked.

'A fasrad.' The robot made no effort to explain. It regarded him without emotion, as if it was not its responsibility to explain anything. 'It will take only a moment.'

'I—' Morris began. He moved back, out of the wind. And the robot, without change of expression, glided past him and into the house.

'Thank you,' it said. It halted in the middle of the living room. 'Would you call your wife, please? I would like to show her the fasrad, also.'

'Sally,' Morris muttered helplessly. 'Come here.'

Sally swept breathlessly into the living room, her breasts quivering with excitement. 'What is it? Oh!' She saw the robot and halted uncertainly. 'Ed, did you order something? Are we buying something?'

'Good evening,' the robot said to her. 'I am going to show you the fasrad. Please be seated. On the couch, if you will. Both together.'

Sally sat down expectantly, her cheeks flushed, eyes bright with wonder and bewilderment. Numbly, Ed seated himself beside her. 'Look,' he muttered thickly. 'What the hell is a fasrad? *What's going on?* I don't want to buy anything!'

'What is your name?' the robot asked him.

'Morris.' He almost choked. 'Ed Morris.'

The robot turned to Sally. 'Mrs Morris.' It bowed slightly. 'I'm glad to meet you, Mr and Mrs Morris. You are the first persons in your neighborhood to see the fasrad. This is the initial demonstration in this area.' Its cold eyes swept the room. 'Mr Morris, you are employed, I assume. Where are you employed?'

'He works on Ganymede,' Sally said dutifully, like a little girl in school. 'For the Terran Metals Development Co.'

The robot digested this information. 'A fasrad will be of value to you.' It eyed Sally. 'What do you do?'

'I'm a tape transcriber at Histo-Research.'

'A fasrad will be of no value in your professional work, but it will be helpful here in the home.' It picked up a table in its powerful steel grippers. 'For example, sometimes an attractive piece of furniture is damaged by a clumsy guest.' The robot smashed the table to bits; fragments of wood and plastic rained down. 'A fasrad is needed.'

Morris leaped helplessly to his feet. He was powerless to halt events; a numbing weight hung over him, as the robot tossed the fragments of table away and selected a heavy floor lamp.

'Oh dear,' Sally gasped. 'That's my best lamp.'

'When a fasrad is possessed, there is nothing to fear.' The robot seized the lamp and twisted it grotesquely. It ripped the shade, smashed the bulbs, then threw away the remnants. 'A situation of this kind can occur from some violent explosion, such as an H-Bomb.'

'For God's sake,' Morris muttered. 'We—'

'An H-Bomb attack may never occur,' the robot continued, 'but in such an event a fasrad is indispensable.' It knelt down and pulled an intricate tube from its waist. Aiming the tube at the floor it atomized a hole five feet in diameter. It stepped back from the yawning pocket. 'I have not extended this tunnel, but you can see a fasrad would save your life in case of attack.'

The word *attack* seemed to set off a new train of reactions in its metal brain.

'Sometimes a thug or hood will attack a person at night,' it continued. Without warning it whirled and drove its fist through the wall. A section of the wall collapsed in a heap of powder and debris. 'That takes care of the thug.' The robot straightened out and peered around the room. 'Often you are too tired in the evening to manipulate the buttons on the stove.' It strode into the kitchen and began punching the stove controls; immense quantities of food spilled in all directions.

'Stop!' Sally cried. 'Get away from my stove!'

'You may be too weary to run water for your bath.' The robot tripped the controls of the tub and water poured down. 'Or you may wish to go right to bed.' It yanked the bed from its concealment and threw it flat. Sally retreated in fright as the robot advanced toward her. 'Sometimes after a hard day at work you are too tired to remove your clothing. In that event—'

'Get out of here!' Morris shouted at it. 'Sally, run and get the cops. The thing's gone crazy. *Hurry.*'

'The fasrad is a necessity in all modern homes,' the robot continued. 'For example, an appliance may break down. The fasrad repairs it instantly.' It seized the automatic humidity control and tore the wiring and replaced it on the wall. 'Sometimes you would prefer not to go to work. The fasrad is permitted by law to occupy your position for a consecutive period not to exceed ten days. If, after that period—'

'Good God,' Morris said, as understanding finally came. 'You're the fasrad.'

'That's right,' the robot agreed. 'Fully Automatic Self-Regulating Android (Domestic). There is also the fasrac (Construction), the fasram (Managerial), the fasras (Soldier), and the fasrab (Bureaucrat). I am designed for home use.'

'You—' Sally gasped. 'You're for sale. You're selling yourself.'

'I am demonstrating myself,' the fasrad, the robot, answered. Its impassive metal eyes were fixed intently on Morris as it continued, 'I am sure, Mr Morris, you would like to own me. I am reasonably priced and fully guaranteed. A full book of instructions is included. I cannot conceive of taking *no* for an answer.'

At half past twelve, Ed Morris still sat at the foot of the bed, one shoe on, the other in his hand. He gazed vacantly ahead. He said nothing.

'For heaven's sake,' Sally complained. 'Finish untying that knot and get into bed; you have to be up at five-thirty.'

Morris fooled aimlessly with the shoelace. After a while he dropped the shoe and tugged at the other one. The house was cold and silent. Outside, the dismal night-wind whipped and lashed at the cedars that grew along the side of the building. Sally lay curled up beneath the radiant-lens, a cigarette between her lips, enjoying the warmth and half-dozing.

In the living room stood the fasrad. It hadn't left. It was still there, was waiting for Morris to buy it.

'Come on!' Sally said sharply. 'What's wrong with you? It fixed all the things it broke; it was just demonstrating itself.' She sighed drowsily. 'It certainly gave me a scare. I thought something had gone wrong with it. They certainly had an inspiration, sending it around to sell itself to people.'

Morris said nothing.

Sally rolled over on her stomach and languidly stubbed out her cigarette. 'That's not so much, is it? Ten thousand gold units, and if we get our friends to buy one we get a five per cent commission. All we have to do is show it. It isn't as if we had to *sell* it. It sells itself.' She giggled. 'They always wanted a product that sold itself, didn't they?'

Morris untied the knot in his shoelace. He slid his shoe back on and tied it tight.

'What are you doing?' Sally demanded angrily. 'You come to bed!' She sat up furiously, as Morris left the room and moved slowly down the hall. 'Where are you going?'

In the living room, Morris switched on the light and sat down facing the fasrad. 'Can you hear me?' he said.

'Certainly,' the fasrad answered. 'I'm never inoperative. Sometimes an emergency occurs at night: a child is sick or an accident takes place. You have no children as yet, but in the event—'

'Shut up,' Morris said, 'I don't want to hear you.'

'You asked me a question. Self-regulating androids are plugged in to a central information exchange. Sometimes a person wishes immediate information; the fasrad is always ready to answer any theoretical or factual inquiry. Anything not metaphysical.'

Morris picked up the book of instructions and thumbed it. The fasrad did thousands of things; it never wore out; it was never at a loss; it couldn't make a mistake. He threw the book away. 'I'm not going to buy you,' he said to it. 'Never. Not in a million years.'

'Oh, yes you are,' the fasrad corrected. 'This is an opportunity you can't afford to miss.' There was calm, metallic confidence in its voice. 'You can't turn me down, Mr Morris. A fasrad is an indispensable necessity in the modern home.'

'Get out of here,' Morris said evenly. 'Get out of my house and don't come back.'

'I'm not your fasrad to order around. Until you've purchased me at the regular list price, I'm responsible only to Self-Regulating Android Inc. Their instructions were to the contrary; I'm to remain with you until you buy me.'

'Suppose I never buy you?' Morris demanded, but in his heart ice formed even as he asked. Already he felt the cold terror of the answer that was coming; there could be no other.

'I'll continue to remain with you,' the fasrad said; 'eventually you'll buy me.' It plucked some withered roses from a vase on the mantel and dropped them into its disposal slot. 'You will see more and more situations in which a fasrad is indispensable. Eventually you'll wonder how you ever existed without one.'

'Is there anything you can't do?'

'Oh, yes; there's a great deal I can't do. But I can do anything *you* can do—and considerably better.'

Morris let out his breath slowly. 'I'd be insane to buy you.'

'You've got to buy me,' the impassive voice answered. The fasrad extended a hollow pipe and began cleaning the carpet. 'I am useful in all situations. Notice how fluffy and free of dust this rug is.' It withdrew the pipe and extended another. Morris coughed and staggered quickly away; clouds of white particles billowed out and filled every part of the room.

'I am spraying for moths,' the fasrad explained.

The white cloud turned to an ugly blue-black. The room faded into ominous darkness; the fasrad was a dim shape moving methodically about in the center. Presently the cloud lifted and the furniture emerged.

'I sprayed for harmful bacteria,' the fasrad said.

It painted the walls of the room and constructed new furniture to go with them. It reinforced the ceiling in the bathroom. It increased the number of heat-vents from the furnace. It put in new electrical wiring. It tore out all the fixtures in the kitchen and assembled more modern ones. It examined Morris' financial accounts and computed his income tax for the following year. It sharpened all the pencils; it caught hold of his wrist and quickly diagnosed his high blood-pressure as psychosomatic.

'You'll feel better after you've turned responsibility over to me,' it explained. It threw out some old soup Sally had been saving. 'Danger of botulism,' it told him. 'Your wife is sexually attractive, but not capable of a high order of intellectualization.'

Morris went to the closet and got his coat.

'Where are you going?' the fasrad asked.

'To the office.'

'At this time of night?'

Morris glanced briefly into the bedroom. Sally was sound asleep under the soothing radiant-lens. Her slim body was rosy pink and healthy, her face free of worry. He closed the front door and hurried down the steps into the darkness. Cold night wind slashed at him as he approached the parking lot. His little commute ship was parked with hundreds of others; a quarter sent the attendant robot obediently after it.

In ten minutes he was on his way to Ganymede.

The fasrad boarded his ship when he stopped at Mars to refuel.

'Apparently you don't understand,' the fasrad said. 'My instructions are to demonstrate myself until you're satisfied. As yet, you're not wholly convinced; further demonstration is necessary.' It passed an intricate web over the controls of the ship until all the dials and meters were in adjustment. 'You should have more frequent servicing.'

It retired to the rear to examine the drive jets. Morris numbly signaled the attendant, and the ship was released from the fuel pumps. He gained speed and the small sandy planet fell behind. Ahead, Jupiter loomed.

'Your jets aren't in good repair,' the fasrad said, emerging from the rear. 'I don't like that knock to the main brake drive. As soon as you land I'll make extensive repair.'

'The Company doesn't mind your doing favors for me?' Morris asked, with bitter sarcasm.

'The Company considers me your fasrad. An invoice will be mailed to you at the end of the month.' The robot whipped out a pen and a pad of forms. 'I'll explain the four easy-payment plans. Ten thousand gold units cash means a three per cent discount. In addition, a number of household items may be traded in—items you won't have further need for. If you wish to divide the purchase in four parts, the first is due at once, and the last in ninety days.'

'I always pay cash,' Morris muttered. He was carefully resetting the route positions on the control board.

'There's no carrying charge for the ninety day plan. For the six month plan there's a six per cent annum charge which will amount to approximately—' It broke off. 'We've changed course.'

'That's right.'

'We've left the official traffic lane.' The fasrad stuck its pen and pad away and hurried to the control board. 'What are you doing? There's a two unit fine for this.'

Morris ignored it. He hung on grimly to the controls and kept his eyes on the viewscreen. The ship was gaining speed rapidly. Warning buoys sounded angrily as he shot past them and into the bleak darkness of space beyond. In a few seconds they had left all traffic behind. They were alone, shooting rapidly away from Jupiter, out into deep space.

The fasrad computed the trajectory. 'We're moving out of the solar system. Toward Centaurus.'

'You guessed it.'

'Hadn't you better call your wife?'

Morris grunted and notched the drive bar farther up. The ship bucked and pitched, then managed to right itself. The jets began to whine ominously. Indicators showed the main turbines were beginning to heat. He ignored them and threw on the emergency fuel supply.

'I'll call Mrs Morris,' the fasrad offered. 'We'll be beyond range in a short while.'

'Don't bother.'

'She'll worry.' The fasrad hurried to the back and examined the jets again. It popped back into the cabin buzzing with alarm. 'Mr Morris, this ship is not equipped for intersystem travel. It's a Class D four-shaft domestic model for home consumption only. It was never made to stand this velocity.'

'To get to Proxima,' Morris answered, 'we need this velocity.'

The fasrad connected its power cables to the control board. 'I can take some of the strain off the wiring system. But unless you rev her back to normal I can't be responsible for the deterioration of the jets.'

'The hell with the jets.'

The fasrad was silent. It was listening intently to the growing whine under them. The whole ship shuddered violently. Bits of paint drifted down. The floor was hot from the grinding shafts. Morris' foot stayed on the throttle. The ship gained more velocity as Sol fell behind. They were out of the charted area. Sol receded rapidly.

'It's too late to vid your wife,' the fasrad said. 'There are three emergency-rockets in the stern; if you want, I'll fire them off in the hope of attracting a passing military transport.'

'Why?'

'They can take us in tow and return us to the Sol system. There's a six hundred gold unit fine, but under the circumstances it seems to me the best policy.'

Morris turned his back to the fasrad and jammed down the throttle with all his weight. The whine had grown to a violent roar. Instruments smashed and cracked. Fuses blew up and down the board. The lights dimmed, faded, then reluctantly came back.

'Mr Morris,' the fasrad said, 'you must prepare for death. The statistical probabilities of turbine explosion are seventy-thirty. I'll do what I can, but the danger-point has already passed.'

Morris returned to the viewscreen. For a time he gazed hungrily up at the growing dot that was the twin star Centaurus. 'They look all right, don't they? Prox is the important one. Twenty planets.' He examined the wildly fluttering instruments. 'How are the jets holding up? I can't tell from these; most of them are burned out.'

The fasrad hesitated. It started to speak, then changed his mind. 'I'll go back and examine them,' it said. It moved to the rear of the ship and disappeared down the short ramp into the thundering, vibrating engine chamber.

Morris leaned over and put out his cigarette. He waited a moment longer, then reached out and yanked the drives full up, the last possible notch on the board.

The explosion tore the ship in half. Sections of hull hurtled around him. He was lifted weightless and slammed into the control board. Metal and plastic rained down on him. Flashing incandescent points winked, faded, and finally died into silence, and there was nothing but cold ash.

The dull *swish-swish* of emergency air-pumps brought consciousness back. He was pinned under the wreckage of the control board; one arm was broken and bent under him. He tried to move his legs but there was no sensation below his waist.

The splintered debris that had been his ship was still hurling toward Centaurus. Hull-sealing equipment was feebly trying to patch the gaping holes. Automatic temperature and grav feeds were thumping spasmodically from self-contained batteries. In the viewscreen the vast flaming bulk of the twin suns grew quietly, inexorably.

He was glad. In the silence of the ruined ship he lay buried beneath the debris, gratefully watching the growing bulk. It was a beautiful sight. He had wanted to see it for a long time. There it was, coming closer each moment. In a day or two the ship would plunge into the fiery mass and be consumed. But he could enjoy this interval; there was nothing to disturb his happiness.

He thought about Sally, sound asleep under the radiant-lens. Would Sally have liked Proxima? Probably not. Probably she would have wanted to go back home as soon as possible. This was something he had to enjoy alone. This was for him only. A vast peace descended over him. He could lie here without stirring, and the flaming magnificence would come nearer and nearer . . .

A sound. From the heaps of fused wreckage something was rising. A twisted, dented shape dimly visible in the flickering glare of the viewscreen. Morris managed to turn his head.

The fasrad staggered to a standing position. Most of its trunk was gone, smashed and broken away. It tottered, then pitched forward on its face with a grinding crash. Slowly it inched its way toward him, then settled to a dismal halt a few feet off. Gears whirred creakily. Relays popped open and shut. Vague, aimless life animated its devastated hulk.

'Good evening,' its shrill, metallic voice grated.

Morris screamed. He tried to move his body but the ruined beams held him tight. He shrieked and shouted and tried to crawl away from it. He spat and wailed and wept.

'I would like to show you a fasrad,' the metallic voice continued. 'Would you call your wife, please? I would like to show her a fasrad, too.'

'Get away!' Morris screamed. 'Get away from me!'

'Good evening,' the fasrad continued, like a broken tape. 'Good evening. Please be seated. I am happy to meet you. What is your name? Thank you. You are the first persons in your neighborhood to see the fasrad. Where are you employed?'

Its dead eye-lenses gaped at him empty and vacant.

'Please be seated,' it said again. 'This will take only a second. Only a second. This demonstration will take only a—'

Introduction by Michael Dinner

Story and Script Title: The Father-Thing

Michael Dinner is an American director, producer, and writer. He is known for his work as an executive producer and director for The Wonder Years and Justified. More recently, Dinner is an executive producer for the popular Amazon series Sneaky Pete.

We all got Daddy issues.

The Father-Thing encompasses the quintessential genre theme of *What does it mean to be human?*

It is a replacement story – a story about humans being replaced by replicated versions. And although it is a premise that exists in other genre fiction, I love the story because it is as much about the invasion of a family as it is about the invasion of the community or the country or the world.

It is told through the eyes of a child – he is the hero of his own story. And it haunts me.

I find the power in Dick's story comes from the question it poses: 'What would you do if the person you love most in the world turns out to be a monster?' It is the story of a boy who, aided by his friends, rises up to fight an unspeakable evil. It is dark. Funny. Scary. Freudian. And extremely emotional:

Among the old leaves and torn-up cardboard, the rotting remains of magazines and curtains, rubbish from the attic his mother had lugged down here with the idea of burning someday. It still looked a little like his father, enough for him to recognize. He had found it — and the sight made him sick at his stomach. He hung onto the barrel and shut his eyes until finally he was able to look again. In the barrel were the remains of his father his real father. Bits the father-thing had no use for. Bits it had discarded.

The approach in adapting the story was relatively simple. I wanted to preserve the emotional core while firmly placing it in my own world.

I have two sons, 11 and 13. I adapted it for them. And I adapted it for my own father.

THE FATHER-THING

'Dinner's ready,' commanded Mrs Walton. 'Go get your father and tell him to wash his hands. The same applies to you, young man.' She carried a steaming casserole to the neatly set table. 'You'll find him out in the garage.'

Charles hesitated. He was only eight years old, and the problem bothering him would have confounded Hillel. 'I—' he began uncertainly.

'What's wrong?' June Walton caught the uneasy tone in her son's voice and her matronly bosom fluttered with sudden alarm. 'Isn't Ted out in the garage? For heaven's sake, he was sharpening the hedge shears a minute ago. He didn't go over to the Andersons', did he? I told him dinner was practically on the table.'

'He's in the garage,' Charles said. 'But he's—talking to himself.'

'Talking to himself!' Mrs Walton removed her bright plastic apron and hung it over the doorknob. 'Ted? Why, he never talks to himself. Go tell him to come in here.' She poured boiling black coffee in the little blue-and-white china cups and began ladling out creamed corn. 'What's wrong with you? Go tell him!'

'I don't know which of them to tell.' Charles blurted out desperately. 'They both look alike.'

June Walton's fingers lost their hold on the aluminum pan; for a moment the creamed corn slushed dangerously. 'Young man—' she began angrily, but at that moment Ted

Walton came striding into the kitchen, inhaling and sniffing and rubbing his hands together.

'Ah,' he cried happily. 'Lamb stew.'

'Beef stew,' June murmured. 'Ted, what were you doing out there?'

Ted threw himself down at his place and unfolded his napkin. 'I got the shears sharpened like a razor. Oiled and sharpened. Better not touch them—they'll cut your hand off.' He was a good-looking man in his early thirties; thick blond hair, strong arms, competent hands, square face and flashing brown eyes. 'Man, this stew looks good. Hard day at the office—Friday, you know. Stuff piles up and we have to get all the accounts out by five. Al McKinley claims the department could handle 20 per cent more stuff if we organized our lunch hours; staggered them so somebody was there all the time.' He beckoned Charles over. 'Sit down and let's go.'

Mrs Walton served the frozen peas. 'Ted,' she said, as she slowly took her seat, 'is there anything on your mind?'

'On my mind?' He blinked. 'No, nothing unusual. Just the regular stuff. Why?'

Uneasily, June Walton glanced over at her son. Charles was sitting bolt-upright at his place, face expressionless, white as chalk. He hadn't moved, hadn't unfolded his napkin or even touched his milk. A tension was in the air; she could feel it. Charles had pulled his chair away from his father's; he was huddled in a tense little bundle as far from his father as possible. His lips were moving, but she couldn't catch what he was saying.

'What is it?' she demanded, leaning toward him.

'*The other one*,' Charles was muttering under his breath. 'The other one came in.'

'What do you mean, dear?' June Walton asked out loud. 'What other one?'

Ted jerked. A strange expression flitted across his face. It vanished at once; but in the brief instant Ted Walton's face lost all familiarity. Something alien and cold gleamed out, a twisting, wriggling mass. The eyes blurred and receded, as an archaic sheen filmed over them. The ordinary look of a tired, middle-aged husband was gone.

And then it was back—or nearly back. Ted grinned and began to wolf down his stew and frozen peas and creamed corn. He laughed, stirred his coffee, kidded and ate. But something terrible was wrong.

'The other one,' Charles muttered, face white, hands beginning to tremble. Suddenly he leaped up and backed away from the table. 'Get away!' he shouted. 'Get out of here!'

'Hey,' Ted rumbled ominously. 'What's got into you?' He pointed sternly at the boy's chair. 'You sit down there and eat your dinner, young man. Your mother didn't fix it for nothing.'

Charles turned and ran out of the kitchen, upstairs to his room. June Walton gasped and fluttered in dismay. 'What in the world—'

Ted went on eating. His face was grim; his eyes were hard and dark. 'That kid,' he grated, 'is going to have to learn a few things. Maybe he and I need to have a little private conference together.'

Charles crouched and listened.

The father-thing was coming up the stairs, nearer and nearer. 'Charles!' it shouted angrily. 'Are you up there?'

He didn't answer. Soundlessly, he moved back into his room and pulled the door shut. His heart was pounding heavily. The father-thing had reached the landing; in a moment it would come in his room.

He hurried to the window. He was terrified; it was already fumbling in the dark hall for the knob. He lifted the window and climbed out on the roof. With a grunt he dropped into the flower garden that ran by the front door, staggered and gasped, then leaped to his feet and ran from the light that streamed out the window, a patch of yellow in the evening darkness.

He found the garage; it loomed up ahead, a black square against the skyline. Breathing quickly, he fumbled in his pocket for his flashlight, then cautiously slid the door up and entered.

The garage was empty. The car was parked out front. To the left was his father's workbench. Hammers and saws on the wooden walls. In the back were the lawnmower, rake, shovel, hoe. A drum of kerosene. License plates nailed up everywhere. Floor was concrete and dirt; a great oil slick stained the center, tufts of weeds greasy and black in the flickering beam of the flashlight.

Just inside the door was a big trash barrel. On top of the barrel were stacks of soggy newspapers and magazines, moldy and damp. A thick stench of decay issued from them as Charles began to move them around. Spiders dropped to the cement and scampered off; he crushed them with his foot and went on looking.

The sight made him shriek. He dropped the flashlight and leaped wildly back. The garage was plunged into instant gloom. He forced himself to kneel down and, for an ageless moment, he groped in the darkness for the light, among the spiders and greasy weeds. Finally he had it again. He managed to turn the beam down into the barrel, down the well he had made by pushing back the piles of magazines.

The father-thing had stuffed it down in the very bottom of the barrel. Among the old leaves and torn-up cardboard, the rotting remains of magazines and curtains, rubbish from the attic his mother had lugged down here with the idea of burning someday. It still looked a little like his father, enough for him to recognize. He had found it—and the sight made him sick at his stomach. He hung onto the barrel and shut his eyes until finally he was able to look again. In the barrel were the remains of his father, his real father. Bits the father-thing had no use for. Bits it had discarded.

He got the rake and pushed it down to stir the remains. They were dry. They cracked and broke at the touch of the rake. They were like a discarded snake skin, flaky and crumbling, rustling at the touch. *An empty skin.* The insides were gone. The important part. This was all that remained, just the brittle, cracking skin, wadded down at the bottom of the trash barrel in a little heap. This was all the father-thing had left; it had eaten the rest. Taken the insides—and his father's place.

A sound.

He dropped the rake and hurried to the door. The father-thing was coming down the path, toward the garage. Its shoes crushed the gravel; it felt its way along uncertainly. 'Charles!' it called angrily. 'Are you in there? Wait'll I get my hands on you, young man!'

His mother's ample, nervous shape was outlined in the bright doorway of the house. 'Ted, please don't hurt him. He's all upset about something.'

'I'm not going to hurt him,' the father-thing rasped; it halted to strike a match. 'I'm just going to have a little talk with him. He needs to learn better manners. Leaving the table like that and running out at night, climbing down the roof—'

Charles slipped from the garage; the glare of the match caught his moving shape, and with a bellow the father-thing lunged forward.

'*Come here!*'

Charles ran. He knew the ground better than the father-thing; it knew a lot, had taken a lot when it got his father's insides, but nobody knew the way like *he* did. He reached the fence, climbed it, leaped into the Andersons' yard, raced past their clothesline, down the path around the side of their house, and out on Maple Street.

He listened, crouched down and not breathing. The father-thing hadn't come after him. It had gone back. Or it was coming around the sidewalk.

He took a deep, shuddering breath. He had to keep moving. Sooner or later it would find him. He glanced right and left, made sure it wasn't watching, and then started off at a rapid dog-trot.

'What do you want?' Tony Peretti demanded belligerently. Tony was fourteen. He was sitting at the table in the oak-paneled Peretti dining room, books and pencils scattered around him, half a ham-and-peanut butter sandwich and a coke beside him. 'You're Walton, aren't you?'

Tony Peretti had a job uncrating stoves and refrigerators after school at Johnson's Appliance Shop, downtown. He was big and blunt-faced. Black hair, olive skin, white teeth. A couple of times he had beaten up Charles; he had beaten up every kid in the neighborhood.

Charles twisted. 'Say, Peretti. Do me a favor?'

'What do you want?' Peretti was annoyed. 'You looking for a bruise?'

Gazing unhappily down, his fists clenched, Charles explained what had happened in short, mumbled words.

When he had finished, Peretti let out a low whistle. 'No kidding.'

'It's true.' He nodded quickly. 'I'll show you. Come on and I'll show you.'

Peretti got slowly to his feet. 'Yeah, show me. I want to see.'

He got his b.b. gun from his room, and the two of them walked silently up the dark street, toward Charles' house. Neither of them said much. Peretti was deep in thought, serious and solemn-faced. Charles was still dazed; his mind was completely blank.

They turned down the Anderson driveway, cut through the back yard, climbed the fence, and lowered themselves cautiously into Charles' back yard. There was no movement. The yard was silent. The front door of the house was closed.

They peered through the living room window. The shades were down, but a narrow crack of yellow streamed out. Sitting on the couch was Mrs Walton, sewing a cotton T-shirt. There was a sad, troubled look on her large face. She worked listlessly, without interest. Opposite her was the father-thing. Leaning back in his father's easy chair, its shoes off, reading the evening newspaper. The TV was on, playing to itself in the corner. A can of beer rested on the arm of the easy chair. The father-thing sat exactly as his own father had sat; it had learned a lot.

'Looks just like him,' Peretti whispered suspiciously. 'You sure you're not bulling me?'

Charles led him to the garage and showed him the trash barrel. Peretti reached his long tanned arms down and carefully pulled up the dry, flaking remains. They spread out, unfolded, until the whole figure of his father was outlined. Peretti laid the remains on the floor and pieced broken parts back into place. The remains were colorless. Almost transparent. An amber yellow, thin as paper. Dry and utterly lifeless.

'That's all,' Charles said. Tears welled up in his eyes. 'That's all that's left of him. The thing has the insides.'

Peretti had turned pale. Shakily, he crammed the remains back in the trash barrel. 'This is really something,' he muttered. 'You say you saw the two of them together?'

'Talking. They looked exactly alike. I ran inside.' Charles wiped the tears away and sniveled; he couldn't hold it back any longer. 'It ate him while I was inside. Then it came in the house. It pretended it was him. But it isn't. It killed him and ate his insides.'

For a moment Peretti was silent. 'I'll tell you something,' he said suddenly. 'I've heard about this sort of thing. It's a bad business. You have to use your head and not get scared. You're not scared, are you?'

'No,' Charles managed to mutter.

'The first thing we have to do is figure out how to kill it.' He rattled his b.b. gun. 'I don't know if this'll work. It must be plenty tough to get hold of your father. He was a big man.' Peretti considered. 'Let's get out of here. It might come back. They say that's what a murderer does.'

They left the garage. Peretti crouched down and peeked through the window again. Mrs Walton had got to her feet. She was talking anxiously. Vague sounds filtered out. The father-thing threw down its newspaper. They were arguing.

'For God's sake!' the father-thing shouted. 'Don't do anything stupid like that.'

'Something's wrong,' Mrs Walton moaned. 'Something terrible. Just let me call the hospital and see.'

'Don't call anybody. He's all right. Probably up the street playing.'

'He's never out this late. He never disobeys. He was terribly upset—afraid of you! I don't blame him.' Her voice broke with misery. 'What's wrong with you? You're so strange.' She moved out of the room, into the hall. 'I'm going to call some of the neighbors.'

The father-thing glared after her until she had disappeared. Then a terrifying thing happened. Charles gasped; even Peretti grunted under his breath.

'Look,' Charles muttered. 'What—'

'Golly,' Peretti said, black eyes wide.

As soon as Mrs Walton was gone from the room, the father-thing sagged in its chair. It became limp. Its mouth fell open. Its eyes peered vacantly. Its head fell forward, like a discarded rag doll.

Peretti moved away from the window. 'That's it,' he whispered. 'That's the whole thing.'

'What is it?' Charles demanded. He was shocked and bewildered. 'It looked like somebody turned off its power.'

'Exactly.' Peretti nodded slowly, grim and shaken. 'It's controlled from outside.'

Horror settled over Charles. 'You mean, something outside our world?'

Peretti shook his head with disgust. 'Outside the house! In the yard. You know how to find?'

'Not very well.' Charles pulled his mind together. 'But I know somebody who's good at finding.' He forced his mind to summon the name. 'Bobby Daniels.'

'That little black kid? Is he good at finding?'

'The best.'

'All right,' Peretti said. 'Let's go get him. We have to find the thing that's outside. That made *it* in there, and keeps it going . . .'

'It's near the garage,' Peretti said to the small, thin-faced Negro boy who crouched beside them in the darkness. 'When it got him, he was in the garage. So look there.'

'In the garage?' Daniels asked.

'*Around* the garage. Walton's already gone over the garage, inside. Look around outside. Nearby.'

There was a small bed of flowers growing by the garage, and a great tangle of bamboo and discarded debris between the garage and the back of the house. The moon had come out; a cold, misty light filtered down over everything. 'If we don't find it pretty soon,' Daniels said, 'I got to go back home. I can't stay up much later.' He wasn't any older than Charles. Perhaps nine.

'All right,' Peretti agreed. 'Then get looking.'

The three of them spread out and began to go over the ground with care. Daniels worked with incredible speed; his thin little body moved in a blur of motion as he crawled among the flowers, turned over rocks, peered under the house, separated stalks of plants, ran his expert hands over leaves and stems, in tangles of compost and weeds. No inch was missed.

Peretti halted after a short time. 'I'll guard. It might be dangerous. The father-thing might come and try to stop us.' He posted himself on the back step with his b.b. gun while Charles and Bobby Daniels searched. Charles worked slowly. He was tired, and his body was cold and numb. It seemed impossible, the father-thing and what had happened to his own father, his real father. But terror spurred him on; what if it happened to his mother, or to him? Or to everyone? Maybe the whole world.

'I found it!' Daniels called in a thin, high voice. 'You all come around here quick!'

Peretti raised his gun and got up cautiously. Charles hurried over; he turned the flickering yellow beam of his flashlight where Daniels stood.

The Negro boy had raised a concrete stone. In the moist, rotting soil the light gleamed on a metallic body. A thin, jointed thing with endless crooked legs was digging frantically. Plated, like an ant; a red-brown bug that rapidly disappeared before their eyes. Its rows of legs scabbed and clutched. The ground gave rapidly under it. Its wicked-looking tail twisted furiously as it struggled down the tunnel it had made.

Peretti ran into the garage and grabbed up the rake. He pinned down the tail of the bug with it. 'Quick! Shoot it with the b.b. gun!'

Daniels snatched the gun and took aim. The first shot tore the tail of the bug loose. It writhed and twisted frantically; its tail dragged uselessly and some of its legs broke off. It was a foot long, like a great millipede. It struggled desperately to escape down its hole.

'Shoot again,' Peretti ordered.

Daniels fumbled with the gun. The bug slithered and hissed. Its head jerked back and forth; it twisted and bit at the rake holding it down. Its wicked specks of eyes gleamed with hatred. For a moment it struck futilely at the rake; then abruptly, without warning, it thrashed in a frantic convulsion that made them all draw away in fear.

Something buzzed through Charles' brain. A loud humming, metallic and harsh, a billion metal wires dancing and vibrating at once. He was tossed about violently by the force; the banging crash of metal made him deaf and confused. He stumbled to his feet and backed off; the others were doing the same, white-faced and shaken.

'If we can't kill it with the gun,' Peretti gasped, 'we can drown it. Or burn it. Or stick a pin through its brain.' He fought to hold onto the rake, to keep the bug pinned down.

'I have a jar of formaldehyde,' Daniels muttered. His fingers fumbled nervously with the b.b. gun. 'How do this thing work? I can't seem to—' Charles grabbed the gun from him. 'I'll kill it.' He squatted down, one eye to the sight, and gripped the trigger. The bug lashed and struggled. Its force-field hammered in his ears, but he hung onto the gun. His finger tightened . . .

'All right, Charles,' the father-thing said. Powerful fingers gripped him, a paralyzing pressure around his wrists. The gun fell to the ground as he struggled futilely. The father-thing shoved against Peretti. The boy leaped away and the bug, free of the rake, slithered triumphantly down its tunnel.

'You have a spanking coming, Charles,' the father-thing droned on. 'What got into you? Your poor mother's out of her mind with worry.'

It had been there, hiding in the shadows. Crouched in the darkness watching them. Its calm, emotionless voice, a dreadful parody of his father's, rumbled close to his ear as it pulled him relentlessly toward the garage. Its cold breath blew in his face, an icy-sweet odor, like decaying soil. Its strength was immense; there was nothing he could do.

'Don't fight me,' it said calmly. 'Come along, into the garage. This is for your own good. I know best, Charles.'

'Did you find him?' his mother called anxiously, opening the back door.

'Yes, I found him.'

'What are you going to do?'

'A little spanking.' The father-thing pushed up the garage door. 'In the garage.' In the half-light a faint smile, humorless and utterly without emotion, touched its lips. 'You go back in the living room, June. I'll take care of this. It's more in my line. You never did like punishing him.'

The back door reluctantly closed. As the light cut off, Peretti bent down and groped for the b.b. gun. The father-thing instantly froze.

'Go on home, boys,' it rasped.

Peretti stood undecided, gripping the b.b. gun.

'Get going,' the father-thing repeated. 'Put down that toy and get out of here.' It moved slowly toward Peretti, gripping

Charles with one hand, reaching toward Peretti with the other. 'No b.b. guns allowed in town, sonny. Your father know you have that? There's a city ordinance. I think you better give me that before—'

Peretti shot it in the eye.

The father-thing grunted and pawed at its ruined eye. Abruptly it slashed out at Peretti. Peretti moved down the driveway, trying to cock the gun. The father-thing lunged. Its powerful fingers snatched the gun from Peretti's hands. Silently, the father-thing mashed the gun against the wall of the house.

Charles broke away and ran numbly off. Where could he hide? It was between him and the house. Already, it was coming back toward him, a black shape creeping carefully, peering into the darkness, trying to make him out. Charles retreated. If there were only some place he could hide . . .

The bamboo.

He crept quickly into the bamboo. The stalks were huge and old. They closed after him with a faint rustle. The father-thing was fumbling in its pocket; it lit a match, then the whole pack flared up. 'Charles,' it said. 'I know you're here, someplace. There's no use hiding. You're only making it more difficult.'

His heart hammering, Charles crouched among the bamboo. Here, debris and filth rotted. Weeds, garbage, papers, boxes, old clothing, boards, tin cans, bottles. Spiders and salamanders squirmed around him. The bamboo swayed with the night wind. Insects and filth.

And something else.

A shape, a silent, unmoving shape that grew up from the mound of filth like some nocturnal mushroom. A white column, a pulpy mass that glistened moistly in the moonlight. Webs covered it, a moldy cocoon. It had vague arms and legs. An indistinct half-shaped head. As yet, the features hadn't formed. But he could tell what it was.

A mother-thing. Growing here in the filth and dampness, between the garage and the house. Behind the towering bamboo.

It was almost ready. Another few days and it would reach maturity. It was still a larva, white and soft and pulpy. But the sun would dry and warm it. Harden its shell. Turn it dark and strong. It would emerge from its cocoon, and one day when his mother came by the garage . . . Behind the mother-thing were other pulpy white larvae, recently laid by the bug. Small. Just coming into existence. He could see where the father-thing had broken off; the place where it had grown. It had matured here. And in the garage, his father had met it.

Charles began to move numbly away, past the rotting boards, the filth and debris, the pulpy mushroom larvae. Weakly, he reached out to take hold of the fence—and scrambled back.

Another one. Another larvae. He hadn't seen this one, at first. It wasn't white. It had already turned dark. The web, the pulpy softness, the moistness, were gone. It was ready. It stirred a little, moved its arm feebly.

The Charles-thing.

The bamboo separated, and the father-thing's hand clamped firmly around the boy's wrist. 'You stay right here,' it said. 'This is exactly the place for you. Don't move.' With its other hand it tore at the remains of the cocoon binding the Charles-thing. 'I'll help it out—it's still a little weak.'

The last shred of moist gray was stripped back, and the Charles-thing tottered out. It floundered uncertainly, as the father-thing cleared a path for it toward Charles.

'This way,' the father-thing grunted. 'I'll hold him for you. When you've fed you'll be stronger.'

The Charles-thing's mouth opened and closed. It reached greedily toward Charles. The boy struggled wildly, but the father-thing's immense hand held him down.

'Stop that, young man,' the father-thing commanded. 'It'll be a lot easier for you if you—'

It screamed and convulsed. It let go of Charles and staggered back. Its body twitched violently. It crashed against the garage, limbs jerking. For a time it rolled and flopped in a dance of agony. It whimpered, moaned, tried to crawl away. Gradually it became quiet. The Charles-thing settled down in a silent heap. It lay stupidly among the bamboo and rotting debris, body slack, face empty and blank.

At last the father-thing ceased to stir. There was only the faint rustle of the bamboo in the night wind.

Charles got up awkwardly. He stepped down onto the cement driveway. Peretti and Daniels approached, wide-eyed and cautious. 'Don't go near it,' Daniels ordered sharply. 'It ain't dead yet. Takes a little while.'

'What did you do?' Charles muttered.

Daniels set down the drum of kerosene with a gasp of relief. 'Found this in the garage. We Daniels, always used kerosene on our mosquitoes, back in Virginia.'

'Daniels poured the kerosene down the bug's tunnel,' Peretti explained, still awed. 'It was his idea.'

Daniels kicked cautiously at the contorted body of the father-thing. 'It's dead, now. Died as soon as the bug died.'

'I guess the other'll die, too,' Peretti said. He pushed aside the bamboo to examine the larvae growing here and there among the debris. The Charles-thing didn't move at all, as Peretti jabbed the end of a stick into its chest. 'This one's dead.'

'We better make sure,' Daniels said grimly. He picked up the heavy drum of kerosene and lugged it to the edge of the bamboo. 'It dropped some matches in the driveway. You get them, Peretti.'

They looked at each other.

'Sure,' Peretti said softly.

'We better turn on the hose,' Charles said. 'To make sure it doesn't spread.'

'Let's get going,' Peretti said impatiently. He was already moving off. Charles quickly followed him and they began searching for the matches, in the moonlit darkness.

Introduction by Matthew Graham

Story Title: The Hood Maker
Script Title: The F Maker

Matthew Graham is a television writer and producer known for creating and writing the television series Life on Mars and Ashes to Ashes. Graham wrote and executive produced the television mini-series Childhood's End, based on the novel by Arthur C. Clarke.

In my formative reading years, from 10 until 18, I devoured as much of the SF oeuvre as I could get my hands on. Which, considering my local library allowed me 5 books every fortnight, was a considerable amount. Asimov, Herbert, Heinlein, Bradbury, Clarke all had a big influence on my imagination. Philip K. Dick was undoubtedly the most challenging and the most thrilling.

PKD drops you from a great height into his world, without explanation or apology. Here in his mind the normal rules do not apply and it's nought to sixty in a millisecond, so keep your wits about you. An opening sentence could easily be something along the lines of 'Catoran Malovich used his echo-scooter to escape through the city. But the Green Brain was close behind.'

OK, I made that one up. But you get my point. We're in and we're running. There was an energy to his prose, at once dense and economical, that propelled me forward and set my pulse keening. PKD knew how to paint a picture in the mind but he also knew that despite the inherent cinematic quality of his work this was Literature, not a smuggled-in screenplay pitch to the movie studios (as so many novelists do today). How ironic, then, that filmmakers line up to adapt his work.

Reading his anthology of short stories, I tended to read too fast. I missed stuff because I was hungry to race through it and start the next. Getting through his stories was like collecting Pokemon. Gotta get 'em all! So I got excited and missed stuff, I was a kid, so sue me. As a consequence, when I read *The Hood Maker*, I missed the point made on the first page that the 'hood' in question, worn by a man named Franklin and designed to protect him from mind-reading, was not in fact an actual hood but a concealed metal headband.

By the time I revisited the story a few years later, I realised my error. But it was too late. The image of a man walking through a crowded city street wearing a hood over his head was burnt into my mind. It seemed so ethereal and so disturbing. At once a brave act of public defiance and announcement of personal identity, and yet also the exact opposite – a way to hide and to be aloof and be secretive. It spoke to the theme of the story – what secrets do we have the right to keep? Should all our thoughts be sacred even if they are dark or dangerous ones? Do I have the right to read your mind if I believe it's in the national interest? Can I hide? Is that wrong?

When I had the great privilege of choosing a story of PKD's to adapt for *Electric Dreams*, I went to *The Hood Maker* and

decided to stick with my original, more childish interpre-
tation. I kept the hoods. Because they disturbed me and
I wanted to find imagery that was disturbing and a little
iconic for the film. And because rightly or erroneously I
had responded to the material in a personal way and felt
that that should be preserved. Because adapting your heroes
is deeply personal. Just as reading their work is. Dick more
than anyone. His work starts as a lecture, becomes a dialogue
and evolves into a relationship.

So enjoy this lecture, conversation and relationship. It will
be fleeting but hopefully stay with you forever. As it did
with me.

THE HOOD MAKER

'A hood!'

'Somebody with a hood!'

Workers and shoppers hurried down the sidewalk, joining the forming crowd. A sallow-faced youth dropped his bike and raced over. The crowd grew, businessmen in gray coats, tired-faced secretaries, clerks and workmen.

'Get him!' The crowd swarmed forward. 'The old man!'

The sallow-faced youth scooped up a rock from the gutter and hurled it. The rock missed the old man, crashing against a store front.

'He's got a hood, all right!'

'Take it away!'

More rocks fell. The old man gasped in fear, trying to push past two soldiers blocking his way. A rock struck him on the back.

'What you got to hide?' The sallow-faced youth ran up in front of him. 'Why you afraid of a probe?'

'He's got something to hide!' A worker grabbed the old man's hat. Eager hands groped for the thin metal band around his head.

'Nobody's got a right to hide!'

The old man fell, sprawling to his hands and knees, umbrella rolling. A clerk caught hold of the hood and tugged. The crowd surged, struggling to get to the metal band. Suddenly the youth gave a cry. He backed off, the hood held up. 'I got it! I got it.' He ran to his bike and pedalled off rapidly, gripping the bent hood.

A robot police car pulled up to the curb, siren screaming. Robot cops leaped out, clearing the mob away.

'You hurt?' They helped the old man up.

The old man shook his head, dazed. His glasses hung from one ear. Blood and saliva streaked his face.

'All right.' The cop's metal fingers released. 'Better get off the street. Inside someplace. For your own good.'

Clearance Director Ross pushed the memo plate away. 'Another one. I'll be glad when the Anti-Immunity Bill is passed.'

Peters glanced up. 'Another?'

'Another person wearing a hood—a probe shield. That makes ten in the last forty-eight hours. They're mailing more out all the time.'

'Mailed, slipped under doors, in pockets, left at desks—countless ways of distribution.'

'If more of them notified us—'

Peters grinned crookedly. 'It's a wonder any of them do. There's a reason why hoods are sent to these people. They're not picked out at random.'

'Why are they picked?'

'They have something to hide. Why else would hoods be sent to them?'

'What about those who *do* notify us?'

'They're afraid to wear them. They pass the hoods on to us—to avoid suspicion.'

Ross reflected moodily. 'I suppose so.'

'An innocent man has no reason to conceal his thoughts. Ninety-nine per cent of the population is glad to have its mind scanned. Most people *want* to prove their loyalty. But this one per cent is guilty of something.'

Ross opened a manila folder and took out a bent metal band. He studied it intently. 'Look at it. Just a strip of some alloy. But it effectively cuts off all probes. The teeps go crazy. It buzzes them when they try to get past. Like a shock.'

'You've sent samples to the lab, of course.'

'No. I don't want any of the lab workers turning out their own hoods. We have trouble enough!'

'Who was this taken from?'

Ross stabbed a button on his desk. 'We'll find out. I'll have the teep make a report.'

The door melted and a lank sallow-faced youth came into the room. He saw the metal band in Ross' hand and smiled, a thin, alert smile. 'You wanted me?'

Ross studied the youth. Blond hair, blue eyes. An ordinary looking kid, maybe a college sophomore. But Ross knew better. Ernest Abbud was a telepathic mutant—a teep. One of several hundred employed by Clearance for its loyalty probes.

Before the teeps, loyalty probes had been haphazard. Oaths, examinations, wire-tappings, were not enough. The theory that each person had to prove his loyalty was fine—as a theory. In practice few people could do it. It looked as if the concept of guilty until proved innocent might have to be abandoned and the Roman law restored.

The problem, apparently insoluble, had found its answer in the Madagascar Blast of 2004. Waves of hard radiation had lapped over several thousand troops stationed in the area. Of those who lived, few produced subsequent progeny. But of the several hundred children born to the survivors of the blast, many showed neural characteristics of a radically new kind. A human mutant had come into being—for the first time in thousands of years.

The teeps appeared by accident. But they solved the most pressing problem the Free Union faced: the detection and punishment of disloyalty. The teeps were invaluable to the Government of the Free Union—and the teeps knew it.

'You got this?' Ross asked, tapping the hood.

Abbud nodded. 'Yes.'

The youth was following his thoughts, not his spoken words. Ross flushed angrily. 'What was the man like?' he demanded harshly. 'The memo plate gives no details.'

'Doctor Franklin is his name. Director of the Federal Resources Commission. Sixty-seven years of age. Here on a visit to a relative.'

'Walter Franklin! I've heard of him.' Ross stared up at Abbud. 'Then you already—'

'As soon as I removed the hood I was able to scan him.'

'Where did Franklin go after the assault?'

'Indoors. Instructed by the police.'

'They arrived?'

'After the hood had been taken, of course. It went perfectly. Franklin was spotted by another telepath, not myself. I was informed Franklin was coming my way. When he reached me I shouted that he was wearing a hood. A crowd collected and others took up the shout. The other telepath arrived and we manipulated the crowd until we were near him. I took the hood myself—and you know the rest.'

Ross was silent for a moment. 'Do you know how he got that hood? Did you scan that?'

'He received it by mail.'

'Does he—'

'He has no idea who sent it or where it came from.'

Ross frowned. 'Then he can't give us any information about them. The senders.'

'The Hood Makers,' Abbud said icily.

Ross glanced quickly up. 'What?'

'The Hood Makers. *Somebody* makes them.' Abbud's face was hard. '*Somebody* is making probe screens to keep us out.'

'And you're sure—'

'Franklin knows nothing! He arrived in the city last night. This morning his mail machine brought the hood. For a time he deliberated. Then he purchased a hat and put it on over the hood. He set out on foot toward his niece's house. We spotted him several minutes later, when he entered range.'

'There seems to be more of them, these days. More hoods being sent out. But you know that.' Ross set his jaw. 'We've got to locate the senders.'

'It'll take time. They apparently wear hoods constantly.' Abbud's face twisted. 'We have to get so damn close! Our scanning range is extremely limited. But sooner or later we'll locate one of them. Sooner or later we'll tear a hood off somebody—and find *him* . . .'

'In the last year five thousand hood-wearers have been detected,' Ross stated. 'Five thousand—and not one of them knows anything. Where the hoods come from or who makes them.'

'When there are more of us, we'll have a better chance,' Abbud said grimly. 'Right now there are too few of us. But eventually—'

'You're going to have Franklin probed, aren't you?' Peters said to Ross. 'As a matter of course.'

'I suppose so.' Ross nodded to Abbud. 'You might as well go ahead on him. Have one of your group run the regular total probe and see if there's anything of interest buried down in his non-conscious neural area. Report the results to me in the usual way.'

Abbud reached into his coat. He brought out a tape spool and tossed it down on the desk in front of Ross. 'Here you are.'

'What's this?'

'The total probe on Franklin. All levels—completely searched and recorded.'

Ross stared up at the youth. 'You—'

'We went ahead with it.' Abbud moved toward the door. 'It's a good job. Cummings did it. We found considerable disloyalty. Mostly ideological rather than overt. You'll probably want to pick him up. When he was twenty-four he found some old books and musical records. He was strongly influenced. The latter part of the tape discusses fully our evaluation of his deviation.'

The door melted and Abbud left.

Ross and Peters stared after him. Finally Ross took the tape spool and put it with the bent metal hood.

'I'll be damned,' Peters said. 'They went ahead with the probe.'

Ross nodded, deep in thought, 'Yeah. And I'm not sure I like it.'

The two men glanced at each other—and knew, as they did so, that outside the office Ernest Abbud was scanning their thoughts.

'Damn it!' Ross said futilely. 'Damn it!'

Walter Franklin breathed rapidly, peering around him. He wiped nervous sweat from his lined face with a trembling hand.

Down the corridor the echoing clang of Clearance agents sounded, growing louder.

He had got away from the mob—spared for a while. That was four hours ago. Now the sun had set and evening was settling over greater New York. He had managed to make his way half across the city, almost to the outskirts—and now a public alarm was out for his arrest.

Why? He had worked for the Free Union Government all his life. He had done nothing disloyal. Nothing, except open the morning mail, find the hood, deliberate about it, and finally put it on. He remembered the small instruction tag:

GREETINGS!

This probe screen is sent to you with compliments of the maker and the earnest hope that it will be of some value to you. Thank you.

Nothing else. No other information. For a long time he had pondered. Should he wear it? He had never done anything. He had nothing to hide—nothing disloyal to the Union. But the thought fascinated him. If he wore the hood his mind would be his own. Nobody could look into it. His mind would belong to him again, private, secret, to think as he wished, endless thoughts for no one else's consumption but his own.

Finally he had made up his mind and put on the hood, fitting his old homburg over it. He had gone outside—and within ten minutes a mob was screaming and yelling around him. And now a general alarm was out for his arrest.

Franklin wracked his brain desperately. What could he do? They could bring him up before a Clearance Board. No accusation would be brought: it would be up to him to clear himself, to prove he was loyal. *Had* he ever done anything wrong? Was there something he had done he was forgetting? He had put on the hood. Maybe that was it. There was some sort of an Anti-Immunity bill up in Congress to make wearing of a probe screen a felony, but it hadn't been passed yet—

The Clearance agents were near, almost on him. He retreated down the corridor of the hotel, glancing desperately around him. A red sign glowed: EXIT. He hurried toward it and down a flight of basement stairs, out onto a dark street. It was bad to be outside, where the mobs were. He had tried to remain indoors as much as possible. But now there was no choice.

Behind him a voice shrilled loudly. Something cut past him, smoking away a section of the pavement. A Slem-ray. Franklin ran, gasping for breath, around a corner and down a side street. People glanced at him curiously as he rushed past.

He crossed a busy street and moved with a surging group of theatergoers. Had the agents seen him? He peered nervously around. None in sight.

At the corner he crossed with the lights. He reached the safety zone in the center, watching a sleek Clearance car cruising toward him. Had it seen him go out to the safety zone? He left the zone, heading toward the curb on the far side. The Clearance car shot suddenly forward, gaining speed. Another appeared, coming the other way.

Franklin reached the curb.

The first car ground to a halt. Clearance agents piled out, swarming up onto the sidewalk.

He was trapped. There was no place to hide. Around him tired shoppers and office workers gazed curiously, their faces devoid of sympathy. A few grinned at him in vacant amusement. Franklin peered frantically around. No place, no door, no person—

A car pulled up in front of him, its doors sliding open. 'Get in.' A young girl leaned toward him, her pretty face urgent. 'Get in, damn it!'

He got in. The girl slammed the doors and the car picked up speed. A Clearance car swung in ahead of them, its sleek bulk blocking the street. A second Clearance car moved in behind them.

The girl leaned forward, gripping the controls. Abruptly the car lifted. It left the street, clearing the cars ahead, gaining altitude rapidly. A flash of violet lit up the sky behind them.

'Get down!' the girl snapped. Franklin sank down in his seat. The car moved in a wide arc, passing beyond the protective columns of a row of buildings. On the ground, the Clearance cars gave up and turned back.

Franklin settled back, mopping his forehead shakily. 'Thanks,' he muttered.

'Don't mention it.' The girl increased the car's speed. They were leaving the business section of the city, moving above the residential outskirts. She steered silently, intent on the sky ahead.

'Who are you?' Franklin asked.

The girl tossed something back to him. 'Put that on.'

A hood. Franklin unfastened it and slipped it awkwardly over his head. 'It's in place.'

'Otherwise they'll get us with a teep scan. We have to be careful all the time.'

'Where are we going?'

The girl turned to him, studying him with calm gray eyes, one hand resting on the wheel. 'We're going to the Hood Maker,' she said. 'The public alarm for you is top priority. If I let you off you won't last an hour.'

'But I don't understand.' Franklin shook his head, dazed. 'Why do they want me? What have I done?'

'You're being framed.' The girl brought the car around in a wide arc, wind whistling shrilly through its struts and fenders. 'Framed by the teeps. Things are happening fast. There's no time to lose.'

The little bald-headed man removed his glasses and held out his hand to Franklin, peering near-sightedly. 'I'm glad to meet you, Doctor. I've followed your work at the Board with great interest.'

'Who are you?' Franklin demanded.

The little man grinned self-consciously. 'I'm James Cutter. The Hood Maker, as the teeps call me. This is our factory.' He waved around the room. 'Take a look at it.'

Franklin gazed around him. He was in a warehouse, an ancient wooden building of the last century. Giant worm-scored beams rose up, dry and cracking. The floor was concrete. Old-fashioned fluorescent lights glinted and flickered from the roof. The walls were streaked with water stains and bulging pipes.

Franklin moved across the room, Cutter beside him. He was bewildered. Everything had happened fast. He seemed to be outside New York, in some dilapidated industrial suburb. Men were working on all sides of him, bent over stampers and moulds. The air was hot. An archaic fan whirred. The warehouse echoed and vibrated with a constant din.

'This—' Franklin murmured. 'This is—'

'This is where we make the hoods. Not very impressive, is it? Later on we hope to move to new quarters. Come along and I'll show you the rest.'

Cutter pushed a side door open and they entered a small laboratory, bottles and retorts everywhere in cluttered confusion. 'We do our research in here. Pure and applied. We've learned a few things. Some we may use, some we hope won't be needed. And it keeps our refugees busy.'

'Refugees?'

Cutter pushed some equipment back and seated himself on a lab table. 'Most of the others are here for the same reason as you. Framed by the teeps. Accused of deviation. But we got to them first.'

'But why—'

'Why were you framed? Because of your position. Director of a Government Department. All these men were prominent—and all were framed by teep probes.' Cutter lit a cigarette, leaning back against the water-stained wall. 'We exist because of a discovery made ten years ago in a Government lab.' He tapped his hood. 'This alloy—opaque to probes. Discovered by accident, by one of these men. Teeps came after him instantly, but he escaped. He made a number of hoods and passed them to other workers in his field. That's how we got started.'

'How many are here?'

Cutter laughed. 'Can't tell you that. Enough to turn out hoods and keep them circulating. To people prominent in Government. People holding positions of authority. Scientists, officials, educators—'

'Why?'

'Because we want to get them first, before the teeps. We got to you too late. A total probe report had *already* been made out on you, before the hood was even in the mail.

'The teeps are gradually getting a stranglehold over the Government. They're picking off the best men, denouncing them and getting them arrested. If a teep says a man is disloyal Clearance has to haul him in. We tried to get a hood to you in time. The report couldn't be passed on to Clearance if you were wearing a hood. But they outsmarted us. They got a mob after you and snatched the hood. As soon as it was off they served the report to Clearance.'

'So that's why they wanted it off.'

'The teeps can't file a framed report on a man whose mind is opaque to probes. Clearance isn't that stupid. The teeps have to get the hoods off. Every man wearing a hood is a man out of bounds. They've managed so far by stirring up mobs—but that's ineffectual. Now they're working on this bill in Congress. Senator Waldo's Anti-Immunity Bill. It would outlaw wearing hoods.' Cutter grinned ironically. 'If a man is innocent why shouldn't he want his mind probed? The bill makes wearing a probe shield a felony. People who receive hoods will turn them over to Clearance. There won't be a man in ten thousand who'll keep his hood, if it means prison and confiscation of property.'

'I met Waldo, once. I can't believe he understands what his bill would do. If he could be made to see—'

'Exactly! If he could be made to see. This bill has to be stopped. If it goes through we're licked. And the teeps are in. Somebody has to talk to Waldo and make him see the situation.' Cutter's eyes were bright. 'You know the man. He'll remember you.'

'What do you mean?'

'Franklin, we're sending you back again—to meet Waldo. It's our only chance to stop the bill. And it has to be stopped.'

The cruiser roared over the Rockies, brush and tangled forest flashing by below. 'There's a level pasture over to the right,' Cutter said. 'I'll set her down, if I can find it.'

He snapped off the jets. The roar died into silence. They were coasting above the hills.

'To the right,' Franklin said.

Cutter brought the cruiser down in a sweeping glide. 'This will put us within walking distance of Waldo's estate. We'll go the rest of the way on foot.' A shuddering growl shook them as the landing fins dug into the ground—and they were at rest.

Around them tall trees moved faintly with the wind. It was midmorning. The air was cool and thin. They were high up, still in the mountains, on the Colorado side.

'What are the chances of our reaching him?' Franklin asked.

'Not very good.'

Franklin started. 'Why? Why not?'

Cutter pushed the cruiser door back and leaped out onto the ground. 'Come on.' He helped Franklin out and slammed the door after him. 'Waldo is guarded. He's got a wall of robots around him. That's why we've never tried before. If it weren't crucial we wouldn't be trying now.'

They left the pasture, making their way down the hill along a narrow weed-covered path. 'What are they doing it for?' Franklin asked. 'The teeps. Why do they want to get power?'

'Human nature, I suppose.'

'*Human* nature?'

'The teeps are no different from the Jacobins, the Roundheads, the Nazis, the Bolsheviks. There's always some group that wants to lead mankind—for its own good, of course.'

'Do the teeps believe that?'

'Most teeps believe they're the natural leaders of mankind. Non-telepathic humans are an inferior species. Teeps are the next step up, *homo superior*. And because they're superior, it's natural they should lead. Make all the decisions for us.'

'And you don't agree,' Franklin said.

'The teeps are different from us—but that doesn't mean they're superior. A telepathic faculty doesn't imply general superiority. The teeps aren't a superior race. They're human beings with a special ability. But that doesn't give them a right to tell us what to do. It's not a new problem.'

'Who should lead mankind, then?' Franklin asked. 'Who should be the leaders?'

'*Nobody* should lead mankind. It should lead itself.' Cutter leaned forward suddenly, body tense.

'We're almost there. Waldo's estate is directly ahead. Get ready. Everything depends on the next few minutes.'

'A few robot guards.' Cutter lowered his binoculars. 'But that's not what's worrying me. If Waldo has a teep nearby, he'll detect our hoods.'

'And we can't take them off.'

'No. The whole thing would be out, passed from teep to teep.' Cutter moved cautiously forward. 'The robots will stop us and demand identification. We'll have to count on your Director's clip.'

They left the bushes, crossing the open field toward the buildings that made up Senator Waldo's estate. They came onto a dirt road and followed it, neither of them speaking, watching the landscape ahead.

'Halt!' A robot guard appeared, streaking toward them across the field 'Identify yourselves!'

Franklin showed his clip. 'I'm Director level. We're here to see the Senator. I'm an old friend.'

Automatic relays clicked as the robot studied the identification clip. 'From the Director level?'

'That's right,' Franklin said, becoming uneasy.

'Get out of the way,' Cutter said impatiently. 'We don't have any time to waste.'

The robot withdrew uncertainly. 'Sorry to have stopped you, sir. The Senator is inside the main building. Directly ahead.'

'All right.' Cutter and Franklin advanced past the robot. Sweat stood out on Cutter's round face. 'We made it,' he murmured. 'Now let's hope there aren't any teeps inside.'

Franklin reached the porch. He stepped slowly up, Cutter behind him. At the door he halted, glancing at the smaller man. 'Shall I—'

'Go ahead.' Cutter was tense. 'Let's get right inside. It's safer.'

Franklin raised his hand. The door clicked sharply as its lens photographed him and checked his image. Franklin prayed silently. If the Clearance alarm had been sent out this far—

The door melted.

'Inside,' Cutter said quickly.

Franklin entered, looking around in the semidarkness. He blinked, adjusting to the dim light of the hall. Somebody was coming toward him. A shape, a small shape, coming rapidly, lithely. Was it Waldo?

A lank, sallow-faced youth entered the hall, a fixed smile on his face. 'Good morning, Doctor Franklin,' he said. He raised his Slem-gun and fired.

Cutter and Ernest Abbud stared down at the oozing mass that had been Doctor Franklin. Neither of them spoke. Finally Cutter raised his hand, his face drained of color.

'Was that necessary?'

Abbud shifted, suddenly conscious of him. 'Why not?' He shrugged, the Slem-gun pointed at Cutter's stomach. 'He was an old man. He wouldn't have lasted long in the protective-custody camp.'

Cutter took out his package of cigarettes and lit up slowly, his eyes on the youth's face. He had never seen Ernest Abbud before. But he knew who he was. He watched the sallow-faced youth kick idly at the remains on the floor.

'Then Waldo is a teep,' Cutter said.

'Yes.'

'Franklin was wrong. He *does* have full understanding of his bill.'

'Of course! The Anti-Immunity Bill is an integral part of our activity.' Abbud waved the snout of the Slem-gun. 'Remove your hood. I can't scan you—and it makes me uneasy.'

Cutter hesitated. He dropped his cigarette thoughtfully to the floor and crushed it underfoot. 'What are you doing here? You usually hang out in New York. This is a long way out here.'

Abbud smiled. 'We picked up Doctor Franklin's thoughts as he entered the girl's car—before she gave him the hood. She waited too long. We got a distinct visual image of her, seen from the back seat, of course. But she turned around to give him the hood. Two hours ago Clearance picked her up. She knew a great deal—our first real contact. We were able to locate the factory and round up most of the workers.'

'Oh?' Cutter murmured.

'They're in protective custody. Their hoods are gone—and the supply stored for distribution. The stampers have been dismantled. As far as I know we have all the group. You're the last one.'

'Then does it matter if I keep my hood?'

Abbud's eyes flickered. 'Take it off. I want to scan you— Mister Hood Maker.'

Cutter grunted. 'What do you mean?'

'Several of your men gave us images of you—and details of your trip here. I came out personally, notifying Waldo through our relay system in advance. I wanted to be here myself.'

'Why?'

'It's an occasion. A great occasion.'

'What position do *you* hold?' Cutter demanded.

Abbud's sallow face turned ugly. 'Come on! Off with the hood! I could blast you now. But I want to scan you first.'

'All right. I'll take it off. You can scan me, if you want. Probe all the way down.' Cutter paused, reflecting soberly. 'It's your funeral.'

'What do you mean?'

Cutter removed his hood, tossing it onto a table by the door. 'Well? What do you see? What do I know—*that none of the others knew?*'

For a moment Abbud was silent.

Suddenly his face twitched, his mouth working. The Slem-gun swayed. Abbud staggered, a violent shudder leaping through his lank frame. He gaped at Cutter in rising horror.

'I learned it only recently,' Cutter said. 'In our lab. I didn't want to use it—but you forced me to take off my hood. I always considered the alloy my most important discovery—until this. In some ways, this is even more important. Don't you agree?'

Abbud said nothing. His face was a sickly gray. His lips moved but no sound came.

'I had a hunch—and I played it for all it was worth. I knew you telepaths were born from a single group, resulting from an accident—the Madagascar hydrogen explosion. That made me think. Most mutants, that we know of, are thrown off universally by the species that's reached the mutation stage. Not a single group in one area. The whole world, wherever the species exists.

'Damage to the germ plasma of a specific group of humans is the cause of your existence. You weren't a mutant in the sense that you represented a natural development of the evolutionary process. In no sense could it be said that homo sapiens had reached the mutation stage. So perhaps you weren't a mutant.

'I began to make studies, some biological, some merely statistical.. Sociological research. We began correlating facts on you, on each member of your group we could locate. How old you were. What you were doing for a living. How many were married. Number of children. After a while I came across the facts you're scanning right now.'

Cutter leaned toward Abbud, watching the youth intently.

'You're not a true mutant, Abbud. Your group exists because of a chance explosion. You're different from us because of damage to the reproductive apparatus of your parents. You lack one specific characteristic that true mutants possess.' A faint smile twitched across Cutter's features. 'A lot of you are married. But not one birth has been reported. Not one birth! Not a single teep child! You can't reproduce, Abbud. You're *sterile*, the whole lot of you. When you die there won't be any more.

'You're not mutants. You're freaks!'

Abbud grunted hoarsely, his body trembling. 'I see this, in your mind.' He pulled himself together with an effort. 'And you've kept this secret, have you? You're the only one who knows?'

'Somebody else knows,' Cutter said.

'Who?'

'*You* know. You scanned me. And since you're a teep, all the others—'

Abbud fired, the Slem-gun digging frantically into his own middle. He dissolved, showering in a rain of fragments. Cutter moved back, his hands over his face. He closed his eyes, holding his breath.

When he looked again there was nothing.

Cutter shook his head. 'Too late, Abbud. Not fast enough. Scanning is instant—and Waldo is within range. The relay system . . . And even if they missed you, they can't avoid picking me up.'

A sound. Cutter turned. Clearance agents were moving rapidly into the hall, glancing down at the remains on the floor and up at Cutter.

Director Ross covered Cutter uncertainly, confused and shaken. 'What happened? Where—'

'Scan him!' Peters snapped. 'Get a teep in here quick. Bring Waldo in. Find out what happened.'

Cutter grinned ironically. 'Sure,' he said, nodding shakily. He sagged with relief. 'Scan me. I have nothing to hide. Get a teep in here for a probe—if you can find any . . .'

Introduction by Kalen Egan and Travis Sentell

Story title: Foster, You're Dead
Script Title: Safe & Sound

Travis Sentell is the author of the non-fiction biography In the Shadow of Freedom, and the novel Fluid. His short fiction has appeared in numerous magazines and literary journals.

Kalen Egan has been working for Electric Shepherd Productions since 2007. He is a Co-Executive Producer of the Amazon original series The Man in the High Castle and an Executive Producer of Philip K. Dick's Electric Dreams.

Nearly twenty-five years after his death, Philip K. Dick introduced us to each other.

Like many of PKD's opening sentences, this statement is seemingly impossible, entirely true, and the beginning of a long, strange journey. I (hi, I'm Travis) was leaving my job working for an LA-based literary management company representing the PKD estate, and I (hey, this is Kalen) needed to be trained as a new replacement. Right away, we bonded over a love of books, movies, and – more than anything – Philip K. Dick. Soon after, we began writing screenplays together.

What we've learned after working closely with his material for nearly a decade is that, contrary to popular description, Philip K. Dick wasn't some unique prophet with a direct line to the future. He may seem that way today, but only because the questions that drove him concerned the very core of life itself: *What is human? What is real?* He used science fiction as his personal laboratory, testing the limits of humanity and reality over and over again, seeing where they broke and where they held together. Because those core questions are both perpetually relatable and totally unanswerable, Philip K. Dick's work remains as true and insightful today as it was 60 years ago, and as it will be in another 60 years.

Foster, You're Dead is no exception. Originally published in 1955 and ostensibly about Cold War anxiety, the story first struck us as a clever, cynical study of corporate entities exploiting youthful anxiety for profit. But tucked just under the surface of social commentary, we saw a deeply honest depiction of human beings and human relationships. There was a very real father and a very real son, each with believable and achingly true reactions to an unfair world, whose relationship was being torn apart because their subjective points of view were irreconcilable – the father, desperate not to cave to societal pressure, and the son, desperate to conform. We know this situation. We know these people. Perhaps we are them, or have been, or will be. Like so much of Dick's work, *Foster, You're Dead* tells us that safety is more than mere survival. It tells us that tribal instincts can trump blood relations, that consumer gadgets can be as much about cultural identification as functional assistance or protection, and that adolescents stepping outside of their bubbles need more than simple reassurance. So much in the story feels relevant because the instincts and emotions remain so very familiar.

We wrote our adaptation for *Electric Dreams* during the ascension and election of a man riding a new wave of American populism, and found that we couldn't escape at least a half dozen unintended resonances. Cultural fears involving foreign invaders, personal security, perceived loss of cultural status, ideological gaps between generations . . . Every news cycle sent new, unexpected reverberations through our fictional adaptation, none of which we'd set out to address, but all of which were becoming an inextricable part of the story. But of course, that's the thing – Philip K. Dick's work will always be relevant, because he saw the world and the people around him so clearly. He thought and wrote about humanity with extraordinary precision, and though external circumstances are constantly shifting, these fundamental human attributes remain terrifyingly, beautifully stagnant. The cynicism holds up, but so does the empathy, and in the world of PKD, these two attributes go hand in hand, supporting and combatting each other in equal measure.

Of course, he snuck all this in under the guise of pulp science fiction, baiting us into believing that maybe this is all just fantasy. Only once the story is over, and we take another look at the world around us, do we realize: *It's all completely true.*

FOSTER, YOU'RE DEAD

School was agony, as always. Only today it was worse. Mike Foster finished weaving his two watertight baskets and sat rigid, while all around him the other children worked. Outside the concrete-and-steel building the late-afternoon sun shone cool. The hills sparkled green and brown in the crisp autumn air. In the overhead sky a few NATS circled lazily above the town.

The vast, ominous shape of Mrs Cummings, the teacher, silently approached his desk. 'Foster, are you finished?'

'Yes, ma'am,' he answered eagerly. He pushed the baskets up. 'Can I leave now?'

Mrs Cummings examined his baskets critically. 'What about your trap-making?' she demanded.

He fumbled in his desk and brought out his intricate small-animal trap. 'All finished, Mrs Cummings. And my knife, it's done, too.' He showed her the razor-edged blade of his knife, glittering metal he had shaped from a discarded gasoline drum. She picked up the knife and ran her expert finger doubtfully along the blade.

'Not strong enough,' she stated. 'You've oversharpened it. It'll lose its edge the first time you use it. Go down to the main weapons-lab and examine the knives they've got there. Then hone it back some and get a thicker blade.'

'Mrs Cummings,' Mike Foster pleaded, 'could I fix it *tomorrow*? Could I leave right now, please?'

Everybody in the classroom was watching with interest. Mike Foster flushed; he hated to be singled out and made conspicuous, but he *had* to get away. He couldn't stay in school one minute more.

Inexorable, Mrs Cummings rumbled, 'Tomorrow is digging day. You won't have time to work on your knife.'

'I will' he assured her quickly. 'After the digging.'

'No, you're not too good at digging.' The old woman was measuring the boy's spindly arms and legs. 'I think you better get your knife finished today. And spend all day tomorrow down at the field.'

'What's the use of digging?' Mike Foster demanded, in despair.

'Everybody has to know how to dig,' Mrs Cummings answered patiently. Children were snickering on all sides; she shushed them with a hostile glare. 'You all know the importance of digging. When the war begins the whole surface will be littered with debris and rubble. If we hope to survive we'll have to dig down, won't we? Have any of you ever watched a gopher digging around the roots of plants? The gopher knows he'll find something valuable down there under the surface of the ground. We're all going to be little brown gophers. We'll all have to learn to dig down in the rubble and find the good things, because that's where they'll be.'

Mike Foster sat miserably plucking his knife, as Mrs Cummings moved away from his desk and up the aisle. A few children grinned contemptuously at him, but nothing penetrated his haze of wretchedness. Digging wouldn't do him any good. When the bombs came he'd be killed instantly. All the vaccination shots up and down his arms, on his thighs and buttocks, would be of no use. He had wasted his allowance money: Mike Foster wouldn't be alive to catch any of the bacterial plagues. Not unless—

He sprang up and followed Mrs Cummings to her desk. In an agony of desperation he blurted, 'Please, I have to leave. I have to do something.'

Mrs Cummings' tired lips twisted angrily. But the boy's fearful eyes stopped her. 'What's wrong?' she demanded. 'Don't you feel well?'

The boy stood frozen, unable to answer her. Pleased by the tableau, the class murmured and giggled until Mrs Cummings rapped angrily on her desk with a writer. 'Be quiet,' she snapped. Her voice softened a shade. 'Michael, if you're not functioning properly, go downstairs to the psyche clinic. There's no point trying to work when your reactions are conflicted. Miss Groves will be glad to optimum you.'

'No,' Foster said.

'Then what is it?'

The class stirred. Voices answered for Foster; his tongue was stuck with misery and humiliation. 'His father's an anti-P,' the voices explained. 'They don't have a shelter and he isn't registered in Civic Defense. His father hasn't even contributed to the NATS. They haven't done anything.'

Mrs Cummings gazed up in amazement at the mute boy. 'You don't have a shelter?'

He shook his head.

A strange feeling filled the woman. 'But—' She had started to say, *But you'll die up here.* She changed it to 'But where'll you go?'

'Nowhere,' the mild voices answered for him. 'Everybody else'll be down in their shelters and he'll be up here. He even doesn't have a permit for the school shelter.'

Mrs Cummings was shocked. In her dull, scholastic way she had assumed every child in the school had a permit to the elaborate subsurface chambers under the building. But of course not. Only children whose parents were part of CD, who contributed to arming the community. And if Foster's father was an anti-P . . .

'He's afraid to sit here,' the voices chimed in calmly. 'He's afraid it'll come while he's sitting here, and everybody else will be safe down in the shelter.'

He wandered slowly along, hands deep in his pockets, kicking at dark stones on the sidewalk. The sun was setting. Snub-nosed commute rockets were unloading tired people, glad to be home from the factory strip a hundred miles to the west. On the distant hills something flashed: a radar tower revolving silently in the evening gloom. The circling NATS had increased in number. The twilight hours were the most dangerous; visual observers couldn't spot high-speed missiles coming in close to the ground. Assuming the missiles came.

A mechanical news-machine shouted at him excitedly as he passed. War, death, amazing new weapons developed at home and abroad. He hunched his shoulders and continued on, past the little concrete shells that served as houses, each exactly alike, sturdy reinforced pillboxes. Ahead of him bright neon signs glowed in the settling gloom: the business district, alive with traffic and milling people.

Half a block from the bright cluster of neons he halted. To his right was a public shelter, a dark tunnel-like entrance with a mechanical turnstile glowing dully. Fifty cents admission. If he was here, on the street, and he had fifty cents, he'd be all right. He had pushed down into public shelters many times, during the practice raids. But other times, hideous, nightmare times that never left his mind, he hadn't had the fifty cents. He had stood mute and terrified, while people pushed excitedly past him; and the shrill shrieks of the sirens thundered everywhere.

He continued slowly, until he came to the brightest blotch of light, the great, gleaming showrooms of General Electronics, two blocks long, illuminated on all sides, a vast square of pure color and radiation. He halted and examined for the millionth time the fascinating shapes, the display that always drew him to a hypnotized stop whenever he passed.

In the center of the vast room was a single object. An elaborate pulsing blob of machinery and support struts, beams and walls and sealed locks. All spotlights were turned on it; huge signs announced its hundred and one advantages—as if there could be any doubt.

THE NEW 1972 BOMBPROOF RADIATION-SEALED
SUBSURFACE SHELTER IS HERE! CHECK THESE
STAR-STUDDED FEATURES:
* automatic descent-lift—jam-proof, self-powered,
e-z locking
* triple-layer hull guaranteed to withstand 5g pressure
without buckling
* A-powered heating and refrigeration system—self-
servicing air-purification network
* three decontamination stages for food and water
* four hygienic stages for pre-burn exposure
* complete antibiotic processing
* e-z payment plan

He gazed at the shelter a long time. It was mostly a big tank, with a neck at one end that was the descent tube, and an emergency escape hatch at the other. It was completely self-contained: a miniature world that supplied its own light, heat, air, water, medicines, and almost inexhaustible food. When fully stocked there were visual and audio tapes, entertainment, beds, chairs, vidscreen, everything that made up the above-surface home. It was, actually, a home below the ground. Nothing was missing that might be needed or enjoyed. A family would be safe, even comfortable, during the most severe H-bomb and bacterial-spray attack.

It cost twenty thousand dollars.

While he was gazing silently at the massive display, one of the salesmen stepped out onto the dark sidewalk, on his way to the cafeteria. 'Hi, sonny,' he said automatically, as he passed Mike Foster. 'Not bad, is it?'

'Can I go inside?' Foster asked quickly. 'Can I go down in it?'

The salesman stopped, as he recognized the boy. 'You're that kid,' he said slowly, 'that damn kid who's always pestering us.'

'I'd like to go down in it. Just for a couple minutes. I won't bust anything—I promise. I won't even touch anything.'

The salesman was young and blond, a good-looking man in his early twenties. He hesitated, his reactions divided. The kid was a pest. But he had a family, and that meant a reasonable prospect. Business was bad; it was late September and the seasonal slump was still on. There was no profit in telling the boy to go peddle his newstapes; but on the other hand it was bad business encouraging small fry to crawl around the merchandise. They wasted time; they broke things; they pilfered small stuff when nobody was looking.

'No dice,' the salesman said. 'Look, send your old man down here. Has he seen what we've got?'

'Yes,' Mike Foster said tightly.

'What's holding him back?' The salesman waved expansively up at the great gleaming display. 'We'll give him a good trade-in on his old one, allowing for depreciation and obsolescence. What model has he got?'

'We don't have any,' Mike Foster said.

The salesman blinked. 'Come again?'

'My father says it's a waste of money. He says they're trying to scare people into buying things they don't need. He says—'

'Your father's an anti-P?'

'Yes,' Mike Foster answered unhappily.

The salesman let out his breath. 'Okay, kid. Sorry we can't do business. It's not your fault.' He lingered. 'What the hell's wrong with him? Does he put on the NATS?'

'No.'

The salesman swore under his breath. A coaster, sliding along, safe because the rest of the community was putting up thirty per cent of its income to keep a constant-defense system going. There were always a few of them, in every town. 'How's your mother feel?' the salesman demanded. 'She go along with him?'

'She says—' Mike Foster broke off. 'Couldn't I go down in it for a little while? I won't bust anything. Just *once*.'

'How'd we ever sell it if we let kids run through it? We're not marking it down as a demonstration model—we've got roped into that too often.' The salesman's curiosity was aroused. 'How's a guy get to be anti-P? He always feel this way, or did he get stung with something?'

'He says they sold people as many cars and washing machines and television sets as they could use. He says NATS and bomb shelters aren't good for anything, so people never get all they can use. He says factories can keep turning out guns and gas masks forever, and as long as people are afraid they'll keep paying for them because they think if they don't they might get killed, and maybe a man gets tired of paying for a new car every year and stops, but he's never going to stop buying shelters to protect his children.'

'You believe that?' the salesman asked.

'I wish we had that shelter,' Mike Foster answered. 'If we had a shelter like that I'd go down and sleep in it every night. It'd be there when we needed it.'

'Maybe there won't be a war,' the salesman said. He sensed the boy's misery and fear, and he grinned good-naturedly down at him. 'Don't worry all the time. You probably watch too many vidtapes—get out and play, for a change.'

'Nobody's safe on the surface,' Mike Foster said. 'We have to be down below. And there's no place I can go.'

'Send your old man around,' the salesman muttered uneasily. 'Maybe we can talk him into it. We've got a lot of time-payment plans. Tell him to ask for Bill O'Neill. Okay?'

Mike Foster wandered away, down the black evening street. He knew he was supposed to be home, but his feet dragged and his body was heavy and dull. His fatigue made him remember what the athletic coach had said the day before, during exercises. They were practicing breath suspension, holding a lungful of air and running. He hadn't done well; the others were still red-faced and racing when he halted, expelled his air, and stood gasping frantically for breath.

'Foster,' the coach said angrily, 'you're dead. You know that? If this had been a gas attack—' He shook his head wearily. 'Go over there and practice by yourself. You've got to do better, if you expect to survive.'

But he didn't expect to survive.

When he stepped up onto the porch of his home, he found the living room lights already on. He could hear his father's voice, and more faintly his mother's, from the kitchen. He closed the door after him and began unpeeling his coat.

'Is that you?' his father demanded. Bob Foster sat sprawled out in his chair, his lap full of tapes and report sheets from his retail furniture store. 'Where have you been? Dinner's been ready half an hour.' He had taken off his coat and rolled up his sleeves. His arms were pale and thin, but muscular. He was tired; his eyes were large and dark, his hair thinning. Restlessly, he moved the tapes around, from one stack to another.

'I'm sorry,' Mike Foster said.

His father examined his pocket watch; he was surely the only man who still carried a watch. 'Go wash our hands. What have you been doing?' He scrutinized his son. 'You look odd. Do you feel all right?'

'I was downtown,' Mike Foster said.

'What were you doing?'

'Looking at the shelters.'

Wordless, his father grabbed up a handful of reports and stuffed them into a folder. His thin lips set; hard lines wrinkled his forehead. He snorted furiously as tapes spilled everywhere; he bent stiffly to pick them up. Mike Foster made no move to help him. He crossed to the closet and gave his coat to the hanger. When he turned away his mother was directing the table of food into the dining room.

They ate without speaking, intent on their food and not looking at each other. Finally his father said, 'What'd you see? Same old dogs, I suppose.'

'There's the new '72 models,' Mike Foster answered.

'They're the same as the '71 models.' His father threw down his fork savagely; the table caught and absorbed it. 'A few new gadgets, some more chrome. That's all.' Suddenly he was facing his son defiantly. 'Right?'

Mike Foster toyed wretchedly with his creamed chicken. 'The new ones have a jam-proof descent lift. You can't get stuck halfway down. All you have to do is get in it, and it does the rest.'

'There'll be one next year that'll pick you up and carry you down. This one'll be obsolete as soon as people buy it. That's what they want—they want you to keep buying. They keep putting out new ones as fast as they can. This isn't 1972, it's still 1971. What's that thing doing out already? Can't they wait?'

Mike Foster didn't answer. He had heard it all before, many times. There was never anything new, only chrome and gadgets; yet the old ones became obsolete, anyhow. His father's argument was loud, impassioned, almost frenzied, but it made no sense. 'Let's get an old one, then,' he blurted out. 'I don't care, any one'll do. Even a secondhand one.'

'No, you want the *new* one. Shiny and glittery to impress the neighbors. Lots of dials and knobs and machinery. How much do they want for it?'

'Twenty thousand dollars.'

His father let his breath out. 'Just like that.'

'They've easy time-payment plans.'

'Sure. You pay for it the rest of your life. Interest, carrying charges, and how long is it guaranteed for?'

'Three months.'

'What happens when it breaks down? It'll stop purifying and decontaminating. It'll fall apart as soon as the three months are over.'

Mike Foster shook his head. 'No. It's big and sturdy.'

His father flushed. He was a small man, slender and light, brittle-boned. He thought suddenly of his lifetime of lost battles, struggling up the hard way, carefully collecting and holding on to something, a job, money, his retail store, bookkeeper to manager, finally owner. 'They're scaring us to keep the wheels going,' he yelled desperately at his wife and son. 'They don't want another depression.'

'Bob,' his wife said, slowly and quietly, 'you have to stop this. I can't stand any more.'

Bob Foster blinked. 'What're you talking about?' he muttered. 'I'm tired. These goddamn taxes. It isn't possible for a little store to keep open, not with the big chains. There ought to be a law.' His voice trailed off. 'I guess I'm through eating.' He pushed away from the table and got to his feet. 'I'm going to lie down on the couch and take a nap.'

His wife's thin face blazed. 'You have to get one! I can't stand the way they talk about us. All the neighbors and the merchants, everybody who knows. I can't go anywhere or do anything without hearing about it. Ever since that day they put up the flag. *Anti-P.* The last in the whole town. Those things circling around up there, and everybody paying for them but us.'

'No,' Bob Foster said. 'I can't get one.'

'Why not?'

'Because,' he answered simply, 'I can't afford it.'

There was silence.

'You've put everything in that store,' Ruth said finally. 'And it's failing anyhow. You're just like a pack-rat, hoarding everything down at that ratty little hole-in-the-wall. Nobody wants wood furniture anymore. You're a relic—a curiosity.' She slammed at the table and it leaped wildly to gather the empty dishes, like a startled animal. It dashed furiously from the room and back into the kitchen, the dishes churning in its washtank as it raced.

Bob Foster sighed wearily. 'Let's not fight. I'll be in the living room. Let me take a nap for an hour or so. Maybe we can talk about it later.'

'Always later,' Ruth said bitterly.

Her husband disappeared into the living room, a small, hunched-over figure, hair scraggly and gray, shoulder blades like broken wings.

Mike got to his feet. 'I'll go study my homework,' he said. He followed after his father, a strange look on his face.

The living room was quiet; the vidset was off and the lamp was down low. Ruth was in the kitchen setting the controls on the stove for the next month's meals. Bob Foster lay stretched out on the couch, his shoes off, his head on a pillow. His face was gray with fatigue. Mike hesitated for a moment and then said, 'Can I ask you something?'

His father grunted and stirred, opened his eyes. 'What?'

Mike sat down facing him. 'Tell me again how you gave advice to the President.'

His father pulled himself up. 'I didn't give any advice to the President. I just talked to him.'

'Tell me about it.'

'I've told you a million times. Every once in a while, since you were a baby. You were with me.' His voice softened, as he remembered. 'You were just a toddler—we had to carry you.'

'What did he look like?'

'Well,' his father began, slipping into a routine he had worked out and petrified over the years, 'he looked about like he does in the vidscreen. Smaller, though.'

'Why was he here?' Mike demanded avidly, although he knew every detail. The President was his hero, the man he most admired in all the world. 'Why'd he come all the way out here to *our* town?'

'He was on a tour.' Bitterness crept into his father's voice. 'He happened to be passing through.'

'What kind of a tour?'

'Visiting towns all over the country.' The harshness increased. 'Seeing how we were getting along. Seeing if we had bought enough NATS and bomb shelters and plague shots and gas masks and radar networks to repel attack. The General Electronics Corporation was just beginning to put up its big showrooms and displays—everything bright and glittering and expensive. The first defense equipment available for home purchase.' His lips twisted.

'All on easy-payment plans. Ads, posters, searchlights, free gardenias and dishes for the ladies.'

Mike Foster's breath panted in his throat. 'That was the day we got our Preparedness Flag,' he said hungrily. 'That was the day he came to give us our flag. And they ran it up on the flagpole in the middle of the town, and everybody was there yelling and cheering.'

'You remember that?'

'I—think so. I remember people and sounds. And it was hot. It was June, wasn't it?'

'June 10, 1965. Quite an occasion. Not many towns had the big green flag, then. People were still buying cars and TV sets. They hadn't discovered those days were over. TV sets and cars are good for something—you can only manufacture and sell so many of them.'

'He gave *you* the flag, didn't he?'

'Well, he gave it to all us merchants. The Chamber of Commerce had it arranged. Competition between towns, see who can buy the most the soonest. Improve our town and at the same time stimulate business. Of course, the way they put it, the idea was if we had to *buy* our gas masks and bomb shelters we'd take better care of them. As if we ever damaged telephones and sidewalks. Or highways, because the whole state provided them. Or armies. Haven't there always been armies? Hasn't the government always organized its people for defense? I guess defense costs too much. I guess they save a lot of money, cut down the national debt by this.'

'Tell me what he said,' Mike Foster whispered.

His father fumbled for his pipe and lit it with trembling hands. 'He said, *"Here's your flag, boys. You've done a good job."*' Bob Foster choked, as acrid pipe fumes guzzled up. 'He was red-faced, sunburned, not embarrassed. Perspiring and grinning. He knew how to handle himself. He knew a lot of first names. Told a funny joke.'

The boy's eyes were wide with awe. 'He came all the way out here, and you talked to him.'

'Yeah,' his father said. 'I talked to him. They were all yelling and cheering. The flag was going up, the big green Preparedness Flag.'

'You said—'

'I said to him, "*Is that all you brought us? A strip of green cloth?*"' Bob Foster dragged tensely on his pipe. 'That was when I became an anti-P. Only I didn't know it at the time. All I knew was we were on our own, except for a strip of green cloth. We should have been a country, a whole nation, one hundred and seventy million people working together to defend ourselves. And instead, we're a lot of separate little towns, little walled forts. Sliding and slipping back to the Middle Ages. Raising our separate armies—'

'Will the President ever come back?' Mike asked.

'I doubt it. He was—just passing through.'

'If he comes back,' Mike whispered, tense and not daring to hope, 'can we go *see* him? Can we *look* at him?'

Bob Foster pulled himself up to a sitting position. His bony arms were bare and white; his lean face was drab with weariness. And resignation. 'How much was the damn thing you saw?' he demanded hoarsely. 'That bomb shelter?'

Mike's heart stopped beating. 'Twenty thousand dollars.'

'This is Thursday. I'll go down with you and your mother next Saturday.' Bob Foster knocked out his smoldering, half-lit pipe. 'I'll get it on the easy-payment plan. The fall buying season is coming up soon. I usually do good—people buy wood furniture for Christmas gifts.' He got up abruptly from the couch. 'Is it a deal?'

Mike couldn't answer; he could only nod.

'Fine,' his father said, with desperate cheerfulness. 'Now you won't have to go down and look at it in the window.'

★

The shelter was installed—for an additional two hundred dollars—by a fast-working team of laborers in brown coats with the words GENERAL ELECTRONICS stitched across their backs. The back yard was quickly restored, dirt and shrubs spaded in place, the surface smoothed over, and the bill respectfully slipped under the front door. The lumbering delivery truck, now empty, clattered off down the street and the neighborhood was again silent.

Mike Foster stood with his mother and a small group of admiring neighbors on the back porch of the house. 'Well,' Mrs Carlyle said finally, 'now you've got a shelter. The best there is.'

'That's right,' Ruth Foster agreed. She was conscious of the people around her; it had been some time since so many had shown up at once. Grim satisfaction filled her gaunt frame, almost resentment. 'It certainly makes a difference,' she said harshly.

'Yes,' Mr Douglas from down the street agreed. 'Now you have some place to go.' He had picked up the thick book of instructions the laborers had left. 'It says here you can stock it for a whole year. Live down there twelve months without coming up once.' He shook his head admiringly. 'Mine's an old '69 model. Good for only six months. I guess maybe—'

'It's still good enough for us,' his wife cut in, but there was a longing wistfulness in her voice. 'Can we go down and peek at it, Ruth? It's all ready, isn't it?'

Mike made a strangled noise and moved jerkily forward. His mother smiled understandingly. 'He has to go down there first. He gets first look at it—it's really for him, you know.'

Their arms folded against the chill September wind, the group of men and women stood waiting and watching, as the boy approached the neck of the shelter and halted a few steps in front of it.

He entered the shelter carefully, almost afraid to touch anything. The neck was big for him; it was built to admit a full grown man. As soon as his weight was on the descent lift it dropped beneath him. With a breathless *whoosh* it plummeted down the pitch-black tube to the body of the shelter. The lift slammed hard against its shock absorbers and the boy stumbled from it. The lift shot back to the surface, simultaneously sealing off the subsurface shelter, an impassable steel-and-plastic cork in the narrow neck.

Lights had come on around him automatically. The shelter was bare and empty; no supplies had yet been carried down. It smelled of varnish and motor grease: below him the generators were throbbing dully. His presence activated the purifying and decontamination systems; on the blank concrete wall meters and dials moved into sudden activity.

He sat down on the floor, knees drawn up, face solemn, eyes wide. There was no sound but that of the generators; the world above was completely cut off. He was in a little self-contained cosmos; everything needed was here—or would be here, soon: food, water, air, things to do. Nothing else was wanted. He could reach out and touch—whatever he needed. He could stay here forever, through all time, without stirring. Complete and entire. Not lacking, not fearing, with only the sound of the generators purring below him, and the sheer, ascetic walls around and above him on all sides, faintly warm, completely friendly, like a living container.

Suddenly he shouted, a loud jubilant shout that echoed and bounced from wall to wall. He was deafened by the reverberation. He shut his eyes tight and clenched his fists. Joy filled him. He shouted again—and let the roar of sound lap over him, his own voice reinforced by the near walls, close and hard and incredibly powerful.

★

The kids in school knew even before he showed up, the next morning. They greeted him as he approached, all of them grinning and nudging each other. 'Is it true your folks got a new General Electronics Model S-72ft?' Earl Peters demanded.

'That's right,' Mike answered. His heart swelled with a peaceful confidence he had never known. 'Drop around,' he said, as casually as he could. 'I'll show it to you.'

He passed on, conscious of their envious faces.

'Well, Mike,' Mrs Cummings said, as he was leaving the classroom at the end of the day. 'How does it feel?'

He halted by her desk, shy and full of quiet pride. 'It feels good,' he admitted.

'Is your father contributing to the NATS?'

'Yes.'

'And you've got a permit for our school shelter?'

He happily showed her the small blue seal clamped around his wrist. 'He mailed a check to the city for everything. He said, "As long as I've gone this far I might as well go the rest of the way."'

'Now you have everything everybody else has.' The elderly woman smiled across at him. 'I'm glad of that. You're now a pro-P, except there's no such term. You're just—like everyone else.'

The next day the news-machines shrilled out the news. The first revelation of the new Soviet bore-pellets.

Bob Foster stood in the middle of the living room, the newstape in his hands, his thin face flushed with fury and despair. 'Goddamn it, it's a plot!' His voice rose in baffled frenzy. 'We just bought the thing and now look. *Look*!' He shoved the tape at his wife. 'You see? I told you!'

'I've seen it,' Ruth said wildly. 'I suppose you think the whole world was just waiting with you in mind. They're always improving weapons, Bob. Last week it was those grain-impregnation flakes. This week it's bore-pellets. You don't expect them to stop the wheels of progress because you finally broke down and bought a shelter, do you?'

The man and woman faced each other. 'What the hell are we going to do?' Bob Foster asked quietly.

Ruth paced back into the kitchen. 'I heard they were going to turn out adaptors.'

'Adaptors! What do you mean?'

'So people won't have to buy new shelters. There was a commercial on the vidscreen. They're going to put some kind of metal grill on the market, as soon as the government approves it. They spread it over the ground and it intercepts the bore-pellets. It screens them, makes them explode on the surface, so they can't burrow down to the shelter.'

'How much?'

'They didn't say.'

Mike Foster sat crouched on the sofa, listening. He had heard the news at school. They were taking their test on berry-identification, examining encased samples of wild berries to distinguish the harmless ones from the toxic, when the bell had announced a general assembly. The principal read them the news about the bore-pellets and then gave a routine lecture on emergency treatment of a new variant of typhus, recently developed.

His parents were still arguing. 'We'll have to get one,' Ruth Foster said calmly. 'Otherwise it won't make any difference whether we've got a shelter or not. The bore-pellets were specifically designed to penetrate the surface and seek out warmth. As soon as the Russians have them in production—'

'I'll get one,' Bob Foster said. 'I'll get an anti-pellet grill and whatever else they have. I'll buy everything they put on the market. I'll never stop buying.'

'It's not as bad as that.'

'You know, this game has one real advantage over selling people cars and TV sets. With something like this we *have* to buy. It isn't a luxury, something big and flashy to impress the neighbors, something we could do without. If we don't buy this we die. They always said the way to sell something was create anxiety in people. Create a sense of insecurity— tell them they smell bad or look funny. But this makes a joke out of deodorant and hair oil. You can't escape this. If you don't buy, *they'll kill you*. The perfect sales-pitch. Buy or die—new slogan. Have a shiny new General Electronics H-bomb shelter in your back yard or be slaughtered.'

'Stop talking like that!' Ruth snapped.

Bob Foster threw himself down at the kitchen table. 'All right. I give up. I'll go along with it.'

'You'll get one? I think they'll be on the market by Christmas.'

'Oh, yes,' Foster said. 'They'll be out by Christmas,' There was a strange look on his face. 'I'll buy one of the damn things for Christmas, and so will everybody else.'

The GEC grill-screen adaptors were a sensation.

Mike Foster walked slowly along the crowd-packed December street, through the late-afternoon twilight. Adaptors glittered in every store window All shapes and sizes, for every kind of shelter. All prices, for every pocket-book. The crowds of people were gay and excited, typical Christmas crowds, shoving good-naturedly, loaded down with packages and heavy overcoats. The air was white with gusts of sweeping snow. Cars nosed cautiously along the jammed streets. Lights and neon displays, immense glowing store windows gleamed on all sides.

His own house was dark and silent. His parents weren't home yet. Both of them were down at the store working; business had been bad and his mother was taking the place of one of the clerks. Mike held his hand up to the code-key, and the front door let him in. The automatic furnace had kept the house warm and pleasant. He removed his coat and put away his schoolbooks.

He didn't stay in the house long. His heart pounding with excitement, he felt his way out the back door and started onto the back porch.

He forced himself to stop, turn around, and reenter the house. It was better if he didn't hurry things. He had worked out every moment of the process, from the first instant he saw the low hinge of the neck reared up hard and firm against the evening sky. He had made a fine art of it; there was no wasted motion. His procedure had been shaped, molded until it was a beautiful thing. The first overwhelming sense of *presence* as the neck of the shelter came around him. Then the blood-freezing rush of air as the descent-lift hurtled down all the way to the bottom.

And the grandeur of the shelter itself.

Every afternoon, as soon as he was home, he made his way down into it, below the surface, concealed and protected in its steel silence, as he had done since the first day. Now the chamber was full, not empty. Filled with endless cans of food, pillows, books, vidtapes, audio-tapes, prints on the walls, bright fabrics, textures and colors, even vases of flowers. The shelter was his place, where he crouched curled up, surrounded by everything he needed.

Delaying things as long as possible, he hurried back through the house and rummaged in the audio-tape file. He'd sit down in the shelter until dinner, listening to *Wind in the Willows*. His parents knew where to find him; he was always down there. Two hours of uninterrupted happiness, alone by himself in the shelter. And then when dinner was over he would hurry back down, to stay until time for bed. Sometimes late at night, when his parents were sound asleep, he got quietly up and made his way outside, to the shelter-neck, and down into its silent depths. To hide until morning.

He found the audio-tape and hurried through the house, out onto the back porch and into the yard. The sky was a bleak gray, shot with streamers of ugly black clouds. The lights of the town were coming on here and there. The yard was cold and hostile. He made his way uncertainly down the steps—and froze.

A vast yawning cavity loomed. A gaping mouth, vacant and toothless, fixed open to the night sky. There was nothing else. The shelter was gone.

He stood for an endless time, the tape clutched in one hand, the other hand on the porch railing. Night came on; the dead hole dissolved in darkness. The whole world gradually collapsed into silence and abysmal gloom. Weak stars came out; lights in nearby houses came on fitfully, cold and faint. The boy saw nothing. He stood unmoving, his body rigid as stone, still facing the great pit where the shelter had been.

Then his father was standing beside him. 'How long have you been here?' his father was saying. 'How long, Mike? Answer me!'

With a violent effort Mike managed to drag himself back. 'You're home early,' he muttered.

'I left the store early on purpose. I wanted to be here when you—got home.'

'It's gone.'

'Yes.' His father's voice was cold, without emotion. 'The shelter's gone. I'm sorry, Mike. I called them and told them to take it back.'

'Why?'

'I couldn't pay for it. Not this Christmas, with those grills everyone's getting. I can't compete with them.' He broke off and then continued wretchedly, 'They were damn decent. They gave me back half the money I put in.' His voice twisted ironically. 'I knew if I made a deal with them before Christmas I'd come out better. They can resell it to somebody else.'

Mike said nothing.

'Try to understand,' his father went on harshly. 'I had to throw what capital I could scrape together into the store. I have to keep it running. It was either give up the shelter or the store. And if I gave up the store—'

'Then we wouldn't have anything.'

His father caught hold of his arm. 'Then we'd have to give up the shelter, too.' His thin, strong fingers dug in spasmodically. 'You're growing up—you're old enough to understand. We'll get one later, maybe not the biggest, the most expensive, but something. It was a mistake, Mike. I couldn't swing it, not with the goddamn adaptor things to buck. I'm keeping up the NAT payments, though. And your school tab. I'm keeping that going. This isn't a matter of principle,' he finished desperately. 'I can't help it. Do you understand, Mike? *I had to do it.*'

Mike pulled away.

'Where are you going?' His father hurried after him. 'Come back here!' He grabbed for his son frantically, but in the gloom he stumbled and fell. Stars blinded him as his head smashed into the edge of the house; he pulled himself up painfully and groped for some support.

When he could see again, the yard was empty. His son was gone.

'Mike!' he yelled. 'Where are you?'

There was no answer. The night wind blew clouds of snow around him, a think bitter gust of chilled air. Wind and darkness, nothing else.

Bill O'Neill wearily examined the clock on the wall. It was nine thirty: he could finally close the doors and lock up the big dazzling store. Push the milling, murmuring throngs of people outside and on their way home.

'Thank God,' he breathed, as he held the door open for the last old lady, loaded down with packages and presents. He threw the code bolt in place and pulled down the shade. 'What a mob. I never saw so many people.'

'All done,' Al Conners said, from the cash register. 'I'll count the money—you go around and check everything. Make sure we got all of them out.'

O'Neill pushed his blond hair back and loosened his tie. He lit a cigarette gratefully, then moved around the store, checking light switches, turning off the massive GEC displays and appliances. Finally he approached the huge bomb shelter that took up the center of the floor.

He climbed the ladder to the neck and stepped onto the lift. The lift dropped with a *whoosh* and a second later he stepped out in the cavelike interior of the shelter.

In one corner Mike Foster sat curled up in a tight heap, his knees drawn up against his chin, his skinny arms wrapped around his ankles. His face was pushed down; only his ragged brown hair showed. He didn't move as the salesman approached him, astounded.

'Jesus!' O'Neill exclaimed. 'It's that kid.'

Mike said nothing. He hugged his legs tighter and buried his head as far down as possible.

'What the hell are you doing down here?' O'Neill demanded, surprised and angry. His outrage increased. 'I thought your folks got one of these.' Then he remembered. 'That's right. We had to repossess it.'

Al Conners appeared from the descent-lift. 'What's holding you up? Let's get out of here and—' He saw Mike and broke off. 'What's he doing down here? Get him out and let's go.'

'Come on, kid,' O'Neill said gently. 'Time to go home.'

Mike didn't move.

The two men looked at each other. 'I guess we're going to have to drag him out,' Conners said grimly. He took off his coat and tossed it over a decontamination fixture. 'Come on. Let's get it over with.'

It took both of them. The boy fought desperatley, without sound, clawing and struggling and tearing at them with his fingernails, kicking them, slashing at them, biting them when they grabbed him. They half-dragged, half-carried him to the descent-lift and pushed him into it long enough to activate the mechanism. O'Neill rode up with him; Conners came immediately after. Grimly, efficiently, they bundled the boy to the front door, threw him out, and locked the bolts after him.

'Wow,' Conners gasped, sinking down against the counter. His sleeve was torn and his cheek was cut and gashed. His glasses hung from one ear; his hair was rumpled and he was exhausted. 'Think we ought to call the cops? There's something wrong with that kid.'

O'Neill stood by the door, panting for breath and gazing out into the darkness. He could see the boy sitting on the pavement. 'He's still out there,' he muttered. People pushed by the boy on both sides. Finally one of them stopped and got him up. The boy struggled away, and then disappeared into the darkness. The larger figure picked up its packages, hesitated a moment, and then went on. O'Neill turned away. 'What a hell of a thing.' He wiped his face with his handkerchief. 'He sure put up a fight.'

'What was the matter with him? He never said anything, not a goddamn word.'

'Christmas is a hell of a time to repossess something,' O'Neill said. He reached shakily for his coat. 'It's too bad. I wish they could have kept it.'

Conners shrugged. 'No tickie, no laundry.'

'Why the hell can't we give them a deal? Maybe—' O'Neill struggled to get the word out. 'Maybe sell the shelter wholesale, to people like that.'

Conners glared at him angrily. '*Wholesale*? And then everybody wants it wholesale. It wouldn't be fair—and how long would we stay in business? How long would GEC last that way?'

'I guess not very long,' O'Neill admitted moodily.

'Use your head.' Conners laughed sharply. 'What you need is a good stiff drink. Come on in the back closet—I've got a fifty of Haig and Haig in a drawer back there. A little something to warm you up, before you go home. That's what you need.'

Mike Foster wandered aimlessly along the dark street, among the crowds of shoppers hurrying home. He saw nothing; people pushed against him but he was unaware of them. Lights, laughing people, the honking of car horns, the clang of signals. He was blank, his mind empty and dead. He walked automatically, without consciousness or feeling.

To his right a garish neon sign winked and glowed in the deepening night shadows. A huge sign, bright and colorful.

PEACE ON EARTH GOOD WILL TO MEN
PUBLIC SHELTER ADMISSION 50c

Introduction by Jessica Mecklenburg

Story and Script Title: Human Is

Jessica Mecklenburg is a writer and producer, best known for her work on the hit Netflix series Stranger Things. Mecklenburg also worked as a supervising producer and writer for Resurrection and Being Mary Jane. She just wrapped season one of Gypsy for Universal Television and Netflix, on which she served as a Co-Executive Producer.

I've always responded to Philip K. Dick's evocative prophecies and deep, sometimes disturbing psychological journeys. Resounding themes and metaphors reside in his spare language. But Jill Herrick's plight in *Human Is* resonated with me profoundly. Her palpable longing to connect with her husband, Lester, on a more emotional level struck a chord I suspect many feel while reading it. This was the genius of Philip K. Dick: setting forth an existential truth against cruel, provocative and cutting edge circumstances.

In *Human Is* Earth is called Terra. It's more militaristic than we've ever known because the elements we need to survive come with the ultimate price tag: our species or theirs. While our characters struggle with the ethical implications of intergalactic warfare, the true stakes of *Human Is* remain emotional and universal.

In looking to adapt *Human Is* for the *Electric Dreams* series, the challenge was in updating Jill and Lester's world without altering the longing, disconnection, and ultimately beauty of our leads' growing attachment following Lester's return from Rexor IV. So much of *Human Is* feels relevant, if not crucial, to our understanding of today's world. In fact, it's astounding how essential Philip K. Dick's work feels. While the time period of the original story is not specified, the story has a timeless quality. We chose to set our version in 2520. I reimagined Jill and Lester, calling them Vera and Silas, while retaining as much of the nuance and honest emotion of Philip K. Dick's original story as possible.

Human Is explores the very real question, 'What does it mean to be human?' Without giving too much away, throughout production, we referred to Silas after his return from Rexor IV as 'Silas Rex'. The irony is that in Latin, 'Rex' means 'King'. *Human Is* is a quintessential Philip K. Dick story as it is paradoxically both a cautionary tale and deeply hopeful. Silas Rex represents the possible future of humanity. For as evolution, innovation and technology inevitably collide, a fundamental truth remains: to be human is to love.

HUMAN IS

Jill Herrick's blue eyes filled with tears. She gazed at her husband in unspeakable horror. 'You're—you're hideous!' she wailed.

Lester Herrick continued working, arranging heaps of notes and graphs in precise piles.

'Hideous,' he stated, 'is a value judgment. It contains no factual information.' He sent a report tape on Centauran parasitic life whizzing through the desk scanner. 'Merely an opinion. An expression of emotion, nothing more.'

Jill stumbled back to the kitchen. Listlessly, she waved her hand to trip the stove into activity. Conveyor belts in the wall hummed to life, hurrying the food from the underground storage lockers for the evening meal.

She turned to face her husband one last time. 'Not even a *little* while?' she begged. 'Not even—'

'Not even for a month. When he comes you can tell him. If you haven't the courage, I'll do it. I can't have a child running around here. I have too much work to do. This report on Betelgeuse XI is due in ten days.' Lester dropped a spool on Fomalhautan fossil implements into the scanner. 'What's the matter with your brother? Why can't he take care of his own child?'

Jill dabbed at swollen eyes. 'Don't you understand? I *want* Gus here! I begged Frank to let him come. And now you—'

'I'll be glad when he's old enough to be turned over to the Government.' Lester's thin face twisted in annoyance. 'Damn it, Jill, isn't dinner ready yet? It's been ten minutes! What's wrong with that stove?'

'It's almost ready.' The stove showed a red signal light. The robant waiter had come out of the wall and was waiting expectantly to take the food.

Jill sat down and blew her small nose violently. In the living room, Lester worked on unperturbed. His work. His research. Day after day. Lester was getting ahead; there was no doubt of that. His lean body was bent like a coiled spring over the tape scanner, cold gray eyes taking in the information feverishly, analyzing, appraising, his conceptual faculties operating like well-greased machinery.

Jill's lips trembled in misery and resentment. Gus—little Gus. How could she tell him? Fresh tears welled up in her eyes. Never to see the chubby little fellow again. He could never come back—because his childish laughter and play bothered Lester. Interfered with his research.

The stove clicked to green. The food slid out, into the arms of the robant. Soft chimes sounded to announce dinner.

'I hear it,' Lester grated. He snapped off the scanner and got to his feet. 'I suppose he'll come while we're eating.'

'I can vid Frank and ask—'

'No. Might as well get it over with.' Lester nodded impatiently to the robant. 'All right. Put it down.' His thin lips set in an angry line. 'Damn it, don't dawdle! I want to get back to my work!'

Jill bit back the tears.

Little Gus came trailing into the house as they were finishing dinner.

Jill gave a cry of joy. 'Gussie!' She ran to sweep him up in her arms. 'I'm so glad to see you!'

'Watch out for my tiger,' Gus muttered. He dropped his little gray kitten onto the rug and it rushed off, under the couch. 'He's hiding.'

Lester's eyes flickered as he studied the little boy and the tip of gray tail extending from under the couch.

'Why do you call it a tiger? It's nothing but an alley cat.'

Gus looked hurt. He scowled. 'He's a tiger. He's got stripes.'

'Tigers are yellow and a great deal bigger. You might as well learn to classify things by their correct names.'

'Lester, please—' Jill pleaded

'Be quiet,' her husband said crossly. 'Gus is old enough to shed childish illusions and develop a realistic orientation. What's wrong with the psych testers? Don't they straighten this sort of nonsense out?'

Gus ran and snatched up his tiger. 'You leave him alone!'

Lester contemplated the kitten. A strange, cold smile played about his lips. 'Come down to the lab some time, Gus. We'll show you lots of cats. We use them in our research. Cats, guinea pigs, rabbits—'

'Lester!' Jill gasped. 'How can you!'

Lester laughed thinly. Abruptly he broke off and returned to his desk. 'Now clear out of here. I have to finish these reports. And don't forget to tell Gus.'

Gus got excited. 'Tell me what?' His cheeks flushed. His eyes sparkled. 'What is it? Something for me? A *secret*?'

Jill's heart was like lead. She put her hand heavily on the child's shoulder. 'Come on, Gus. We'll go sit out in the garden and I'll tell you. Bring—bring your tiger.'

A click. The emergency vidsender lit up. Instantly Lester was on his feet. 'Be quiet!' He ran to the sender, breathing rapidly. 'Nobody speak!'

Jill and Gus paused at the door. A confidential message was sliding from the slot into the dish. Lester grabbed it up and broke the seal. He studied it intently.

'What is it?' Jill asked. 'Anything bad?'

'Bad?' Lester's face shone with a deep inner glow. 'No, not bad at all.' He glanced at his watch. 'Just time. Let's see, I'll need—'

'What is it?'

'I'm going on a trip. I'll be gone two or three weeks. Rexor IV is into the charted area.'

'Rexor IV? You're going there?' Jill clasped her hands eagerly. 'Oh, I've always wanted to see an old system, old ruins and cities! Lester, can I come along? Can I go with you? We never took a vacation, and you always promised—'

Lester Herrick stared at his wife in amazement. 'You?' he said. '*You* go along?' He laughed unpleasantly. 'Now hurry and get my things together. I've been waiting for this a long time.' He rubbed his hands together in satisfaction. 'You can keep the boy here until I'm back. But no longer. Rexor IV! I can hardly wait!'

'You have to make allowances,' Frank said. 'After all, he's a scientist.'

'I don't care,' Jill said. 'I'm leaving him. As soon as he gets back from Rexor IV. I've made up my mind.'

Her brother was silent, deep in thought. He stretched his feet out, onto the lawn of the little garden. 'Well, if you leave him you'll be free to marry again. You're still classed as sexually adequate, aren't you?'

Jill nodded firmly. 'You bet I am. I wouldn't have any trouble. Maybe I can find somebody who likes children.'

'You think a lot of children,' Frank perceived. 'Gus loves to go visit you. But he doesn't like Lester. Les needles him.'

'I know. This past week has been heaven, with him gone.' Jill patted her soft blonde hair, blushing prettily. 'I've had fun. Makes me feel alive again.'

'When'll he be back?'

'Any day.' Jill clenched her small fists. 'We've been married five years and every year it's worse. He's so—so inhuman. Utterly cold and ruthless. Him and his work. Day and night.'

'Les is ambitious. He wants to get to the top in his field.' Frank lit a cigarette lazily. 'A pusher. Well, maybe he'll do it. What's he in?'

'Toxicology. He works out new poisons for the Military. He invented the copper sulphate skin-lime they used against Callisto.'

'It's a small field. Now take me.' Frank leaned contentedly against the wall of the house. 'There are thousands of Clearance lawyers. I could work for years and never create a ripple. I'm content just to be. I do my job. I enjoy it.'

'I wish Lester felt that way.'

'Maybe he'll change.'

'He'll *never* change,' Jill said bitterly. 'I know that, now. That's why I've made up my mind to leave him. He'll always be the same.'

Lester Herrick came back from Rexor IV a different man. Beaming happily, he deposited his anti-gray suitcase in the arms of the waiting robant. 'Thank you.'

Jill gasped speechlessly. 'Les! What—'

Lester moved his hat, bowing a little. 'Good day, my dear. You're looking lovely. Your eyes are clear and blue. Sparkling like some virgin lake, fed by mountain streams.' He sniffed. 'Do I smell a delicious repast warming on the hearth?'

'Oh, Lester.' Jill blinked uncertainly, faint hope swelling in her bosom. 'Lester, what's happened to you? You're so—so different.'

'Am I, my dear?' Lester moved about the house, touching things and sighing. 'What a dear little house. So sweet and friendly. You don't know how wonderful it is to be here. Believe me.'

'I'm afraid to believe it,' Jill said.

'Believe what?'

'That you mean all this. That you're not the way you were. The way you've always been.'

'What way is that?'

'Mean. Mean and cruel.'

'I?' Lester frowned, rubbing his lip. 'Hmm. Interesting.' He brightened. 'Well, that's all in the past. What's for dinner? I'm faint with hunger.'

Jill eyed him uncertainly as she moved into the kitchen. 'Anything you want, Lester. You know our stove covers the maximum select-list.'

'Of course.' Lester coughed rapidly. 'Well, shall we try sirloin steak, medium, smothered in onions? With mushroom sauce. And white rolls. With hot coffee. Perhaps ice cream and apple pie for dessert.'

'You never seemed to care much about food,' Jill said thoughtfully.

'Oh?'

'You always said you hoped eventually they'd make intravenous intake universally applicable.' She studied her husband intently. 'Lester, what's happened?'

'Nothing. Nothing at all.' Lester carelessly took his pipe out and lit it rapidly, somewhat awkwardly. Bits of tobacco drifted to the rug. He bent nervously down and tried to pick them up again. 'Please go about your tasks and don't mind me. Perhaps I can help you prepare—that is, can I do anything to help?'

'No,' Jill said. 'I can do it. You go ahead with your work, if you want.'

'Work?'

'Your research. In toxins.'

'Toxins!' Lester showed confusion. 'Well, for heaven's sake! Toxins. Devil take it!'

'What, dear?'

'I mean, I really feel too tired, just now. I'll work later.'
Lester moved vaguely around the room. 'I think I'll just
sit and enjoy being home again. Off that awful Rexor IV.'

'Was it awful?'

'Horrible.' A spasm of disgust crossed Lester's face. 'Dry
and dead. Ancient. Squeezed to a pulp by wind and sun. A
dreadful place, my dear.'

'I'm sorry to hear that. I always wanted to visit it.'

'Heaven forbid!' Lester cried feelingly. 'You stay right
here, my dear. With me. The—the two of us.' His eyes
wandered around the room. 'Two, yes. Terra is a wonderful
planet. Moist and full of life.' He beamed happily. 'Just
right.'

'I don't understand it,' Jill said.

'Repeat all the things you remember,' Frank said. His
robot pencil poised itself alertly. 'The changes you've noticed
in him. I'm curious.'

'Why?'

'No reason. Go on. You say you sensed it right away?
That he was different?'

'I noticed it at once. The expression on his face. Not
that hard, practical look. A sort of mellow look. Relaxed.
Tolerant. A sort of calmness.'

'I see,' Frank said. 'What else?'

Jill peered nervously through the back door into the house.
'He can't hear us, can he?'

'No. He's inside playing with Gus. In the living room.
They're Venusian otter-men today. Your husband built an
otter slide down at his lab. I saw him unwrapping it.'

'His talk.'

'His what?'

'The way he talks. His choice of words. Words he never used before. Whole new phrases. Metaphors. I never heard him use a metaphor in all our five years together. He said metaphors were inexact. Misleading. And—'

'And what?' The pencil scratched busily.

'And they're *strange* words. Old words. Words you don't hear any more.'

'Archaic phraseology?' Frank asked tensely.

'Yes.' Jill paced back and forth across the small lawn, her hands in the pockets of her plastic shorts. 'Formal words. Like something—'

'Something out of a book?'

'Exactly! You've noticed it?'

'I noticed it,' Frank's face was grim. 'Go on.'

Jill stopped pacing. 'What's on your mind? Do you have a theory?'

'I want to know more facts.'

She reflected. 'He plays. With Gus. He plays and jokes. And he—he eats.'

'Didn't he eat before?'

'Not like he does now. Now he *loves* food. He goes in the kitchen and tries endless combinations. He and the stove get together and cook up all sorts of weird things.'

'I thought he'd put on weight.'

'He's gained ten pounds. He eats, smiles and laughs. He's constantly polite.' Jill glanced away coyly. 'He's even— romantic! He always said *that* was irrational. And he's not interested in his work. His research in toxins.'

'I see.' Frank chewed his lip. 'Anything more?'

'One thing puzzles me very much. I've noticed it again and again.'

'What is it?'

'He seems to have strange lapses of—'

A burst of laughter. Lester Herrick, eyes bright with merriment, came rushing out of the house, little Gus close behind.

'We have an announcement!' Lester cried.

'An announzelmen,' Gus echoed.

Frank folded his notes up and slid them into his coat pocket. The pencil hurried after them. He got slowly to his feet. 'What is it?'

'You make it,' Lester said, taking little Gus's hand and leading him forward.

Gus's plump face screwed up in concentration. 'I'm going to come live with you,' he stated. Anxiously he watched Jill's expression. 'Lester says I can. Can I? Can I, Aunt Jill?'

Her heart flooded with incredible joy. She glanced from Gus to Lester. 'Do you—do you really mean it?' Her voice was almost inaudible.

Lester put his arm around her, holding her close to him. 'Of course, we mean it,' he said gently. His eyes were warm and understanding. 'We wouldn't tease you, my dear.'

'No teasing!' Gus shouted excitedly. 'No more teasing!' He and Lester and Jill drew close together. 'Never again!'

Frank stood a little way off, his face grim. Jill noticed him and broke away abruptly. 'What is it?' she faltered. 'Is anything—'

'When you're quite finished,' Frank said to Lester Herrick, 'I'd like you to come with me.'

A chill clutched Jill's heart. 'What is it? Can I come, too?'

Frank shook his head. He moved toward Lester ominously. 'Come on, Herrick. Let's go. You and I are going to take a little trip.'

The three Federal Clearance Agents took up positions a few feet from Lester Herrick, vibro-tubes gripped alertly.

Clearance Director Douglas studied Herrick for a long time. 'You're sure?' he said finally.

'Absolutely,' Frank stated.

'When did he get back from Rexor IV?'

'A week ago.'

'And the change was noticeable at once?'

'His wife noticed it as soon as she saw him. There's no doubt it occurred on Rexor.' Frank paused significantly. 'And you know what that means.'

'I know.' Douglas walked slowly around the seated man, examining him from every angle.

Lester Herrick sat quietly, his coat neatly folded across his knee. He rested his hands on his ivory-topped cane, his face calm and expressionless. He wore a soft gray suit, a subdued necktie, French cuffs, and shiny black shoes. He said nothing.

'Their methods are simple and exact,' Douglas said. 'The original psychic contents are removed and stored—in some sort of suspension. The interjection of the substitute contents is instantaneous. Lester Herrick was probably poking around the Rexor city ruins, ignoring the safety precautions—shield or manual screen—and they got him.'

The seated man stirred. 'I'd like very much to communicate with Jill,' he murmured. 'She surely is becoming anxious.'

Frank turned away, face choked with revulsion. 'God. It's still pretending.'

Director Douglas restrained himself with the greatest effort. 'It's certainly an amazing thing. No physical changes. You could look at it and never know.' He moved toward the seated man, his face hard. 'Listen to me, whatever you call yourself. Can you understand what I say?'

'Of course,' Lester Herrick answered.

'Did you really think you'd get away with it? We caught the others—the ones before you. All ten of them. Even before they got here.' Douglas grinned coldly. 'Vibro-rayed them one after another.'

The color left Lester Herrick's face. Sweat came out on his forehead. He wiped it away with a silk handkerchief from his breast pocket. 'Oh?' he murmured.

'You're not fooling us. All Terra is alerted for you Rexorians. I'm surprised you got off Rexor at all. Herrick must have been extremely careless. We stopped the others aboard ship. Fried them out in deep space.'

'Herrick had a private ship,' the seated man murmured. 'He bypassed the check station going in. No record of his arrival existed. He was never checked.'

'*Fry it!*' Douglas grated. The three Clearance agents lifted their tubes, moving forward.

'No.' Frank shook his head. 'We can't. It's a bad situation.'

'What do you mean? Why can't we? We fried the others—'

'They were caught in deep space. This is Terra. Terran law, not military law, applies.' Frank waved toward the seated man. 'And it's in a human body. It comes under regular civil laws. We've got to *prove* it's not Lester Herrick—that it's a Rexorian infiltrator. It's going to be tough. But it can be done.'

'How?'

'His wife. Herrick's wife. Her testimony. Jill Herrick can assert the difference between Lester Herrick and this thing. She knows—and I think we can make it stand up in court.'

It was late afternoon. Frank drove his surface cruiser slowly along. Neither he nor Jill spoke.

'So that's it,' Jill said at last. Her face was gray. Her eyes dry and bright, without emotion. 'I knew it was too good to be true.' She tried to smile. 'It seemed so wonderful.'

'I know,' Frank said. 'It's a terrible damn thing. If only—'

'*Why?*' Jill said. 'Why did he—did it do this? Why did it take Lester's body?'

'Rexor IV is old. Dead. A dying planet. Life is dying out.'

'I remember, now. He—it said something like that. Something about Rexor. That it was glad to get away.'

'The Rexorians are an old race. The few that remain are feeble. They've been trying to migrate for centuries. But their bodies are too weak. Some tried to migrate to Venus—and died instantly. They worked out this system about a century ago.'

'But it knows so much. About us. It speaks our language.'

'Not quite. The changes you mentioned. The odd diction. You see, the Rexorians have only a vague knowledge of human beings. A sort of ideal abstraction, taken from Terran objects that have found their way to Rexor, books mostly. Secondary data like that. The Rexorian idea of Terra is based on centuries-old Terran literature. Romantic novels from our past. Language, custom, manners from old Terran books.

'That accounts for the strange archaic quality to *it*. It had studied Terra, all right. But in an indirect and misleading way.' Frank grinned wryly. 'The Rexorians are two hundred years behind the times—which is a break for us. That's how we're able to detect them.'

'Is this sort of thing—common? Does it happen often? It seems unbelievable.' Jill rubbed her forehead wearily. 'Dreamlike. It's hard to realize that it's actually happened. I'm just beginning to understand what it means.'

'The galaxy is full of alien life forms. Parasitic and destructive entities. Terran ethics don't extend to them. We have to guard constantly against this sort of thing. Lester went in unsuspectingly—and this thing ousted him and took over his body.'

Frank glanced at his sister. Jill's face was expressionless. A stern little face, wide-eyed, but composed. She sat up straight, staring fixedly ahead, her small hands folded quietly in her lap.

'We can arrange it so you won't have to actually appear in court,' Frank went on. 'You can vid a statement and it'll be presented as evidence. I'm certain your statement will do. The Federal courts will help us all they can, but they have to have *some* evidence to go on.'

Jill was silent.

'What do you say?' Frank asked.

'What happens after the court makes its decision?'

'Then we vibro-ray it. Destroy the Rexorian mind. A Terran patrol ship on Rexor IV sends out a party to locate the—er—original contents.'

Jill gasped. She turned toward her brother in amazement. 'You mean—'

'Oh, yes. Lester is alive. In suspension, somewhere on Rexor. In one of the old city ruins. We'll have to force them to give him up. They won't want to, but they'll do it. They've done it before. Then he'll be back with you. Safe and sound. Just like before. And this horrible nightmare you've been living will be a thing of the past.'

'I see.'

'Here we are.' The cruiser pulled to a halt before the imposing Federal Clearance Building. Frank got quickly out, holding the door for his sister. Jill stepped down slowly. 'Okay?' Frank said.

'Okay.'

When they entered the building, Clearance agents led them through the check screens, down the long corridors. Jill's high heels echoed in the ominous silence.

'Quite a place,' Frank observed.

'It's unfriendly.'

'Consider it a glorified police station.' Frank halted. Before them was a guarded door. 'Here we are.'

'Wait.' Jill pulled back, her face twisting in panic. 'I—'

'We'll wait until you're ready.' Frank signaled to the
Clearance agent to leave. 'I understand. It's a bad business.'

Jill stood for a moment, her head down. She took a deep
breath, her small fists clenched. Her chin came up, level and
steady. 'All right.'

'You ready?'

'Yes.'

Frank opened the door. 'Here we are.'

Director Douglas and the three Clearance agents turned
expectantly as Jill and Frank entered. 'Good,' Douglas
murmured, with relief. 'I was beginning to get worried.'

The sitting man got slowly to his feet, picking up his coat.
He gripped his ivory-headed cane tightly, his hands tense.
He said nothing. He watched silently as the woman entered
the room, Frank behind her. 'This is Mrs Herrick,' Frank
said. 'Jill, this is Clearance Director Douglas.'

'I've heard of you,' Jill said faintly.

'Then you know our work.'

'Yes. I know your work.'

'This is an unfortunate business. It's happened before. I
don't know what Frank has told you—'

'He explained the situation.'

'Good.' Douglas was relieved. 'I'm glad of that. It's not
easy to explain. You understand, then, what we want. The
previous cases were caught in deep space. We vibro-tubed
them and got the original contents back. But this time we
must work through legal channels.' Douglas picked up a
vidtape recorder. 'We will need your statement, Mrs Herrick.
Since no physical change has occurred we'll have no direct
evidence to make our case. We'll have only your testimony
of character alteration to present to the court.'

He held the vidtape recorder out. Jill took it slowly.

'Your statement will undoubtedly be accepted by the court.

The court will give us the release we want and then we can go ahead. If everything goes correctly we hope to be able to set up things exactly as they were before.'

Jill was gazing silently at the man standing in the corner with his coat and ivory-headed cane. 'Before?' she said. 'What do you mean?'

'Before the change.'

Jill turned toward Director Douglas. Calmly, she laid the vidtape recorder down on the table. 'What change are you talking about?'

Douglas paled. He licked his lips. All eyes in the room were on Jill. 'The change in *him*.' He pointed at the man.

'Jill!' Frank barked. 'What's the matter with you?' He came quickly toward her. 'What the hell are you doing? You know damn well what change we mean!'

'That's odd,' Jill said thoughtfully. 'I haven't noticed any change.'

Frank and Director Douglas looked at each other. 'I don't get it,' Frank muttered, dazed.

'Mrs Herrick—' Douglas began.

Jill walked over to the man standing quietly in the corner. 'Can we go now, dear?' she asked. She took his arm. 'Or is there some reason why my husband has to stay here?'

The man and woman walked silently along the dark street.

'Come on,' Jill said. 'Let's go home.'

The man glanced at her. 'It's a nice afternoon,' he said. He took a deep breath, filling his lungs. 'Spring is coming—I think. Isn't it?'

Jill nodded.

'I wasn't sure. It's a nice smell. Plants and soil and growing things.'

'Yes.'

'Are we going to walk? Is it far?'

'Not too far.'

The man gazed at her intently, a serious expression on his face. 'I am very indebted to you, my dear,' he said.

Jill nodded.

'I wish to thank you. I must admit I did not expect such a—'

Jill turned abruptly. 'What is your name? Your *real* name.'

The man's gray eyes flickered. He smiled a little, a kind, gentle smile. 'I'm afraid you would not be able to pronounce it. The sounds cannot be formed . . .'

Jill was silent as they walked along, deep in thought. The city lights were coming on all around them. Bright yellow spots in the gloom. 'What are you thinking?' the man asked.

'I was thinking perhaps I will still call you Lester,' Jill said. 'If you don't mind.'

'I don't mind,' the man said. He put his arm around her, drawing her close to him. He gazed down tenderly as they walked through the thickening darkness, between the yellow candles of light that marked the way. 'Anything you wish. Whatever will make you happy.'

Introduction by Travis Beacham

Story and Script Title: Autofac

Travis Beacham is a writer and producer, known for the feature films Pacific Rim and Clash of the Titans. He is currently adapting his own feature script A Killing on Carnival Row into an ongoing television series.

Autofac wasn't the story I was initially planning to adapt, but it was the story that took root and stuck with me and demanded to be adapted. It's an intoxicatingly simple but startlingly fresh premise – this world in which the survivors of some apocalyptic war are trying to shut down an automated factory blindly ravaging the land long after the fall of civilization. You always see stories about malevolent artificial intelligence rebelling against its programming and trying to destroy its creators for some reason. And this story follows a similar path but in the end is something very different. What's brilliant about *Autofac* is that the factory isn't a machine running amok. It's a machine doing exactly what its ingenious but irresponsible creators had built it to do. This machine is not a newly awakened alien intellect bent on the destruction of humanity but rather a kind of monkey's paw that forces us to confront the consequences of our desires as a culture. That, to me, seems not only a touch more realistic than the traditional robot rebellion yarn but also a more timely technological parable in some ways, because it isn't actually about technology. Technology in this story is little more than the ghost of who we used to be, reenacting our mistakes in perpetuity. We're not fighting it. We're fighting ourselves. We're fighting our own nature. It's ultimately about humanity – which is really the mark of a great Philip K. Dick story.

AUTOFAC

I

Tension hung over the three waiting men. They smoked, paced back and forth, kicked aimlessly at weeds growing by the side of the road. A hot noonday sun glared down on brown fields, rows of neat plastic houses, the distant line of mountains to the west.

'Almost time,' Earl Perine said, knotting his skinny hands together. 'It varies according to the load, a half second for every additional pound.'

Bitterly, Morrison answered, 'You've got it plotted? You're as bad as it is. Let's pretend it just *happens* to be late.'

The third man said nothing. O'Neill was visiting from another settlement; he didn't know Perine and Morrison well enough to argue with them. Instead, he crouched down and arranged the papers clipped to his aluminum check-board. In the blazing sun, O'Neill's arms were tanned, furry, glistening with sweat. Wiry, with tangled gray hair, horn-rimmed glasses, he was older than the other two. He wore slacks, a sports shirt and crepe-soled shoes. Between his fingers, his fountain pen glittered, metallic and efficient.

'What're you writing?' Perine grumbled.

'I'm laying out the procedure we're going to employ,' O'Neill said mildly. 'Better to systemize it now, instead of trying at random. We want to know what we tried and what didn't work. Otherwise we'll go around in a circle.

The problem we have here is one of communication; that's how I see it.'

'Communication,' Morrison agreed in his deep, chesty voice. 'Yes, we can't get in touch with the damn thing. It comes, leaves off its load and goes on—there's no contact between us and it.'

'It's a machine,' Perine said excitedly. 'It's dead—blind and deaf.'

'But it's in contact with the outside world,' O'Neill pointed out. 'There has to be some way to get to it. Specific semantic signals are meaningful to it; all we have to do is find those signals. Rediscover, actually. Maybe half a dozen out of a billion possibilities.'

A low rumble interrupted the three men. They glanced up, wary and alert. The time had come.

'Here it is,' Perine said. 'Okay, wise guy, let's see you make one single change in its routine.'

The truck was massive, rumbling under its tightly packed load. In many ways, it resembled conventional human-operated transportation vehicles, but with one exception—there was no driver's cabin. The horizontal surface was a loading stage, and the part that would normally be the headlights and radiator grill was a fibrous spongelike mass of receptors, the limited sensory apparatus of this mobile utility extension.

Aware of the three men, the truck slowed to a halt, shifted gears and pulled on its emergency brake. A moment passed as relays moved into action; then a portion of the loading surface tilted and a cascade of heavy cartons spilled down onto the roadway. With the objects fluttered a detailed inventory sheet.

'You know what to do,' O'Neill said rapidly. 'Hurry up, before it gets out of here.'

Expertly, grimly, the three men grabbed up the deposited cartons and ripped the protective wrappers from them.

Objects gleamed: a binocular microscope, a portable radio, heaps of plastic dishes, medical supplies, razor blades, clothing, food. Most of the shipment, as usual, was food. The three men systematically began smashing objects. In a few minutes, there was nothing but a chaos of debris littered around them.

'That's that,' O'Neill panted, stepping back. He fumbled for his check-sheet. 'Now let's see what it does.'

The truck had begun to move away; abruptly it stopped and backed toward them. Its receptors had taken in the fact that the three men had demolished the dropped-off portion of the load. It spun in a grinding half circle and came around to face its receptor bank in their direction. Up went its antenna; it had begun communicating with the factory. Instructions were on the way.

A second, identical load was tilted and shoved off the truck.

'We failed,' Perine groaned as a duplicate inventory sheet fluttered after the new load. 'We destroyed all that stuff for nothing.'

'What now?' Morrison asked O'Neill. 'What's the next stratagem on our board?'

'Give me a hand.' O'Neill grabbed up a carton and lugged it back to the truck. Sliding the carton onto the platform, he turned for another. The other two men followed clumsily after him. They put the load back onto the truck. As the truck started forward, the last square box was again in place.

The truck hesitated. Its receptors registered the return of its load. From within its works came a low sustained buzzing.

'This may drive it crazy,' O'Neill commented, sweating. 'It went through its operation and accomplished nothing.'

The truck made a short, abortive move toward going on. Then it swung purposefully around and, in a blur of speed, again dumped the load onto the road.

'Get them!' O'Neill yelled. The three men grabbed up the cartons and feverishly reloaded them. But as fast as the cartons were shoved back on the horizontal stage, the truck's grapples tilted them down its far-side ramps and onto the road.

'No use,' Morrison said, breathing hard. 'Water through a sieve.'

'We're licked,' Perine gasped in wretched agreement, 'like always. We humans lose every time.'

The truck regarded them calmly, its receptors blank and impassive. It was doing its job. The planetwide network of automatic factories was smoothly performing the task imposed on it five years before, in the early days of the Total Global Conflict.

'There it goes,' Morrison observed dismally. The truck's antenna had come down; it shifted into low gear and released its parking brake.

'One last try,' O'Neill said. He swept up one of the cartons and ripped it open. From it he dragged a ten-gallon milk tank and unscrewed the lid. 'Silly as it seems.'

'This is absurd,' Perine protested. Reluctantly, he found a cup among the littered debris and dipped it into the milk. 'A kid's game!'

The truck had paused to observe them.

'Do it,' O'Neill ordered sharply. 'Exactly the way we practiced it.'

The three of them drank quickly from the milk tank, visibly allowing the milk to spill down their chins; there had to be no mistaking what they were doing.

As planned, O'Neill was the first. His face twisting in revulsion, he hurled the cup away and violently spat the milk into the road.

'God's sake!' he choked.

The other two did the same; stamping and loudly cursing, they kicked over the milk tank and glared accusingly at the truck.

'It's no good!' Morrison roared.

Curious, the truck came slowly back. Electronic synapses clicked and whirred, responding to the situation; its antenna shot up like a flagpole.

'I think this is it,' O'Neill said, trembling. As the truck watched, he dragged out a second milk tank, unscrewed its lid and tasted the contents. 'The same!' he shouted at the truck. 'It's just as bad!'

From the truck popped a metal cylinder. The cylinder dropped at Morrison's feet; he quickly snatched it up and tore it open.

STATE NATURE OF DEFECT

The instruction sheets listed rows of possible defects, with neat boxes by each; a punch-stick was included to indicate the particular deficiency of the product.

'What'll I check?' Morrison asked. 'Contaminated? Bacterial? Sour? Rancid? Incorrectly labeled? Broken? Crushed? Cracked? Bent? Soiled?'

Thinking rapidly, O'Neill said, 'Don't check any of them. The factory's undoubtedly ready to test and resample. It'll make its own analysis and then ignore us.' His face glowed as frantic inspiration came. 'Write in that blank at the bottom. It's an open space for further data.'

'Write what?'

O'Neill said, 'Write: *the product is thoroughly pizzled.*'

'What's that?' Perine demanded, baffled.

'Write it! It's a semantic garble—the factory won't be able to understand it. Maybe we can jam the works.'

With O'Neill's pen, Morrison carefully wrote that the milk was pizzled. Shaking his head, he resealed the cylinder and returned it to the truck. The truck swept up the milk tanks and slammed its railing tidily into place. With a shriek of tires, it hurtled off. From its slot, a final cylinder bounced; the truck hurriedly departed, leaving the cylinder lying in the dust.

O'Neill got it open and held up the paper for the others to see.

A FACTORY REPRESENTATIVE WILL BE SENT OUT.
BE PREPARED TO SUPPLY COMPLETE DATA ON
PRODUCT DEFICIENCY.

For a moment, the three men were silent. Then Perine began to giggle. 'We did it. We contacted it. We got across.'

'We sure did,' O'Neill agreed. 'It never heard of a product being pizzled.'

Cut into the base of the mountains lay the vast metallic cube of the Kansas City factory. Its surface was corroded, pitted with radiation pox, cracked and scarred from the five years of war that had swept over it. Most of the factory was buried subsurface, only its entrance stages visible. The truck was a speck rumbling at high speed toward the expanse of black metal. Presently an opening formed in the uniform surface; the truck plunged into it and disappeared inside. The entrance snapped shut.

'Now the big job remains,' O'Neill said. 'Now we have to persuade it to close down operations—to shut itself off.'

II

Judith O'Neill served hot black coffee to the people sitting around the living room. Her husband talked while the others listened. O'Neill was as close to being an authority on the autofac system as could still be found.

In his own area, the Chicago region, he had shorted out the protective fence of the local factory long enough to get away with data tapes stored in its posterior brain. The factory, of course, had immediately reconstructed a better type of fence. But he had shown that the factories were not infallible.

'The Institute of Applied Cybernetics,' O'Neill explained, 'had complete control over the network. Blame the war. Blame the big noise along the lines of communication that wiped out the knowledge we need. In any case, the Institute failed to transmit its information to us, so we can't transmit our information to the factories—the news that the war is over and we're ready to resume control of industrial operations.'

'And meanwhile,' Morrison added sourly, 'the damn network expands and consumes more of our natural resources all the time.'

'I get the feeling,' Judith said, 'that if I stamped hard enough, I'd fall right down into a factory tunnel. They must have mines everywhere by now.'

'Isn't there some limiting injunction?' Perine asked nervously. 'Were they set up to expand indefinitely?'

'Each factory is limited to its own operational area,' O'Neill said, 'but the network itself is unbounded. It can go on scooping up our resources forever. The Institute decided it gets top priority; we mere people come second.'

'Will there be *anything* left for us?' Morrison wanted to know.

'Not unless we can stop the network's operations. It's already used up half a dozen basic minerals. Its search teams are out all the time, from every factory, looking everywhere for some last scrap to drag home.'

'What would happen if tunnels from two factories crossed each other?'

O'Neill shrugged. 'Normally, that won't happen. Each factory has its own special section of our planet, its own private cut of the pie for its exclusive use.'

'But it *could* happen.'

'Well, they're raw material-tropic; as long as there's anything left, they'll hunt it down.' O'Neill pondered the idea with growing interest. 'It's something to consider. I suppose as things get scarcer—'

He stopped talking. A figure had come into the room; it stood silently by the door, surveying them all.

In the dull shadows, the figure looked almost human. For a brief moment, O'Neill thought it was a settlement latecomer. Then, as it moved forward, he realized that it was only quasi-human: a functional upright biped chassis, with data-receptors mounted at the top, effectors and proprioceptors mounted in a downward worm that ended in floor-grippers. Its resemblance to a human being was testimony to nature's efficiency; no sentimental imitation was intended.

The factory representative had arrived.

It began without preamble. 'This is a data-collecting machine capable of communicating on an oral basis. It contains both broadcasting and receiving apparatus and can integrate facts relevant to its line of inquiry.'

The voice was pleasant, confident. Obviously it was a tape, recorded by some Institute technician before the war. Coming from the quasi-human shape, it sounded grotesque; O'Neill could vividly imagine the dead young man whose cheerful voice now issued from the mechanical mouth of this upright construction of steel and wiring.

'One word of caution,' the pleasant voice continued. 'It is fruitless to consider this receptor human and to engage it in discussions for which it is not equipped. Although purposeful, it is not capable of conceptual thought; it can only reassemble material already available to it.'

The optimistic voice clicked out and a second voice came on. It resembled the first, but now there were no intonations or personal mannerisms. The machine was utilizing the dead man's phonetic speech-pattern for its own communication.

'Analysis of the rejected product,' it stated, 'shows no foreign elements or noticeable deterioration. The product meets the continual testing-standards employed throughout the network. Rejection is therefore on a basis outside the test area; standards not available to the network are being employed.'

'That's right,' O'Neill agreed. Weighing his words with care, he continued, 'We found the milk substandard. We want nothing to do with it. We insist on more careful output.'

The machine responded presently. 'The semantic content of the term "pizzled" is unfamiliar to the network. It does not exist in the taped vocabulary. Can you present a factual analysis of the milk in terms of specific elements present or absent?'

'No,' O'Neill said warily; the game he was playing was intricate and dangerous. ' "Pizzled" is an overall term. It can't be reduced to chemical constituents.'

'What does "pizzled" signify?' the machine asked. 'Can you define it in terms of alternate semantic symbols?'

O'Neill hesitated. The representative had to be steered from its special inquiry to more general regions, to the ultimate problem of closing down the network. If he could pry it open at any point, get the theoretical discussion started . . .

' "Pizzled," ' he stated, 'means the condition of a product that is manufactured when no need exists. It indicates the rejection of objects on the grounds that they are no longer wanted.'

The representative said, 'Network analysis shows a need of high-grade pasteurized milk-substitute in this area. There is no alternate source; the network controls all the synthetic mammary-type equipment in existence.' It added, 'Original taped instructions describe milk as an essential to human diet.'

O'Neill was being outwitted; the machine was returning the discussion to the specific. 'We've decided,' he said desperately, 'that we don't *want* any more milk. We'd prefer to go without it, at least until we can locate cows.'

'That is contrary to the network tapes,' the representative objected. 'There are no cows. All milk is produced synthetically.'

'Then we'll produce it synthetically ourselves,' Morrison broke in impatiently. 'Why can't we take over the machines? My God, we're not children! We can run our own lives!'

The factory representative moved toward the door. 'Until such time as your community finds other sources of milk supply, the network will continue to supply you. Analytical and evaluating apparatus will remain in this area, conducting the customary random sampling.'

Perine shouted futilely, 'How can we find other sources? You have the whole setup! You're running the whole show!' Following after it, he bellowed, 'You say we're not ready to run things—you claim we're not capable. How do you know? You don't give us a chance! We'll never have a chance!'

O'Neill was petrified. The machine was leaving; its one-track mind had completely triumphed.

'Look,' he said hoarsely, blocking its way. 'We want you to shut down, understand. We want to take over your equipment and run it ourselves. The war's over with. Damn it, you're not needed anymore!'

The factory representative paused briefly at the door. 'The inoperative cycle,' it said, 'is not geared to begin until network production merely duplicates outside production. There is at this time, according to our continual sampling, no outside production. Therefore network production continues.'

Without warning, Morrison swung the steel pipe in his hand. It slashed against the machine's shoulder and burst through the elaborate network of sensory apparatus that made up its chest. The tank of receptors shattered; bits of glass, wiring and minute parts showered everywhere.

'It's a paradox!' Morrison yelled. 'A word game—a semantic game they're pulling on us. The Cyberneticists have it rigged.' He raised the pipe and again brought it down savagely on the unprotesting machine. 'They've got us hamstrung. We're completely helpless.'

The room was in uproar. 'It's the only way,' Perine gasped as he pushed past O'Neill. 'We'll have to destroy them—it's the network or us.' Grabbing down a lamp, he hurled it in the 'face' of the factory representative. The lamp and the intricate surface of plastic burst; Perine waded in, groping blindly for the machine. Now all the people in the room were closing furiously around the upright cylinder, their impotent resentment boiling over. The machine sank down and disappeared as they dragged it to the floor.

Trembling, O'Neill turned away. His wife caught hold of his arm and led him to the side of the room.

'The idiots,' he said dejectedly. 'They can't destroy it; they'll only teach it to build more defenses. They're making the whole problem worse.'

Into the living room rolled a network repair team. Expertly, the mechanical units detached themselves from the half-track mother-bug and scurried toward the mound of struggling humans. They slid between people and rapidly burrowed. A moment later, the inert carcass of the factory representative was dragged into the hopper of the mother-bug. Parts were collected, torn remnants gathered up and carried off. The plastic strut and gear was located. Then the units restationed themselves on the bug and the team departed.

Through the open door came a second factory representative, an exact duplicate of the first. And outside in the hall stood two more upright machines. The settlement had been combed at random by a corps of representatives. Like a horde of ants, the mobile data-collecting machines had filtered through the town until, by chance, one of them had come across O'Neill.

'Destruction of network mobile data-gathering equipment is detrimental to best human interests,' the factory representative informed the roomful of people. 'Raw material intake is at a dangerously low ebb; what basic materials still exist should be utilized in the manufacture of consumer commodities.'

O'Neill and the machine stood facing each other.

'Oh?' O'Neill said softly. 'That's interesting. I wonder what you're lowest on—and what you'd really be willing to fight for.'

Helicopter rotors whined tinnily above O'Neill's head; he ignored them and peered through the cabin window at the ground not far below.

Slag and ruins stretched everywhere. Weeds poked their way up, sickly stalks among which insects scuttled. Here and there, rat colonies were visible: matted hovels constructed of bone and rubble. Radiation had mutated the rats, along with most insects and animals. A little farther, O'Neill identified a squadron of birds pursuing a ground squirrel. The squirrel dived into a carefully prepared crack in the surface of slag and the birds turned, thwarted.

'You think we'll ever have it rebuilt?' Morrison asked. 'It makes me sick to look at it.'

'In time,' O'Neill answered. 'Assuming, of course, that we get industrial control back. And assuming that anything remains to work with. At best, it'll be slow. We'll have to inch out from the settlements.'

To the right was a human colony, tattered scarecrows, gaunt and emaciated, living among the ruins of what had once been a town. A few acres of barren soil had been cleared; drooping vegetables wilted in the sun, chickens wandered listlessly here and there, and a fly-bothered horse lay panting in the shade of a crude shed.

'Ruins-squatters,' O'Neill said gloomily. 'Too far from the network—not tangent to any of the factories.'

'It's their own fault,' Morrison told him angrily. 'They could come into one of the settlements.'

'That was their town. They're trying to do what *we're* trying to do—build up things again on their own. But they're starting now, without tools or machines, with their bare hands, nailing together bits of rubble. And it won't work. We need machines. We can't repair ruins; we've got to start industrial production.'

Ahead lay a series of broken hills, chipped remains that had once been a ridge. Beyond stretched out the titanic ugly sore of an H-bomb crater, half filled with stagnant water and slime, a disease-ridden inland sea.

And beyond that—a glitter of busy motion.

'There,' O'Neill said tensely. He lowered the helicopter rapidly. 'Can you tell which factory they're from?'

'They all look alike to me,' Morrison muttered, leaning over to see. 'We'll have to wait and follow them back, when they get a load.'

'*If* they get a load,' O'Neill corrected.

The autofac exploring crew ignored the helicopter buzzing overhead and concentrated on its job. Ahead of the main truck scuttled two tractors; they made their way up mounds of rubble, probes burgeoning like quills, shot down the far slope and disappeared into a blanket of ash that lay spread over the slag. The two scouts burrowed until only their antennas were visible. They burst up to the surface and scuttled on, their treads whirring and clanking.

'What are they after?' Morrison asked.

'God knows.' O'Neill leafed intently through the papers on his clipboard. 'We'll have to ravell all our back-order slips.'

Below them, the autofac exploring crew disappeared behind. The helicopter passed over a deserted stretch of sand and slag on which nothing moved. A grove of scrub-brush appeared and then, far to the right, a series of tiny moving dots.

A procession of automatic ore carts was racing over the bleak slag, a string of rapidly moving metal trucks that followed one another nose to tail. O'Neill turned the helicopter toward them and a few minutes later it hovered above the mine itself.

Masses of squat mining equipment had made their way to the operations. Shafts had been sunk; empty carts waited in patient rows. A steady stream of loaded carts hurled toward the horizon, dribbling ore after them. Activity and the noise of machines hung over the area, an abrupt center of industry in the bleak wastes of slag.

'Here comes that exploring crew,' Morrison observed, peering back the way they had come. 'You think maybe they'll tangle?' He grinned. 'No, I guess it's too much to hope for.'

'It is this time,' O'Neill answered. 'They're looking for different substances, probably. And they're normally conditioned to ignore each other.'

The first of the exploring bugs reached the line of ore carts. It veered slightly and continued its search; the carts ravelled in their inexorable line as if nothing had happened.

Disappointed, Morrison turned away from the window and swore. 'No use. It's like each doesn't exist for the other.'

Gradually the exploring crew moved away from the line of carts, past the mining operations and over a ridge beyond. There was no special hurry; they departed without having reacted to the ore-gathering syndrome.

'Maybe they're from the same factory,' Morrison said hopefully.

O'Neill pointed to the antennas visible on the major mining equipment. 'Their vanes are turned at a different vector, so these represent two factories. It's going to be hard; we'll have to get it exactly right or there won't be any reaction.' He clicked on the radio and got hold of the monitor at the settlement. 'Any results on the consolidated back-order sheets?'

The operator put him through to the settlement governing offices.

'They're starting to come in,' Perine told him. 'As soon as we get sufficient samplings, we'll try to determine which raw materials which factories lack. It's going to be risky, trying to extrapolate from complex products. There may be a number of basic elements common to the various sublots.'

'What happens when we've identified the missing element?' Morrison asked O'Neill. 'What happens when we've got two tangent factories short on the same material?'

'Then,' O'Neill said grimly, 'we start collecting the material ourselves—even if we have to melt down every object in the settlements.'

III

In the moth-ridden darkness of night, a dim wind stirred, chill and faint. Dense underbrush rattled metallically. Here and there a nocturnal rodent prowled, its senses hyper-alert, peering, planning, seeking food.

The area was wild. No human settlements existed for miles; the entire region had been seared flat, cauterized by repeated H-bomb blasts. Somewhere in the murky darkness, a sluggish trickle of water made its way among slag and weeds, dripping thickly into what had once been an elaborate labyrinth of sewer mains. The pipes lay cracked and broken, jutting up into the night darkness, overgrown with creeping vegetation. The wind raised clouds of black ash that swirled and danced among the weeds. Once an enormous mutant wren stirred sleepily, pulled its crude protective night coat of rags around it and dozed off.

For a time, there was no movement. A streak of stars showed in the sky overhead, glowing starkly, remotely. Earl Perine shivered, peered up and huddled closer to the pulsing heat-element placed on the ground between the three men.

'Well?' Morrison challenged, teeth chattering.

O'Neill didn't answer. He finished his cigarette, crushed it against a mound of decaying slag and, getting out his lighter, lit another. The mass of tungsten—the bait—lay a hundred yards directly ahead of them.

During the last few days, both the Detroit and Pittsburgh factories had run short of tungsten. And in at least one sector, their apparatus overlapped. This sluggish heap represented precision cutting tools, parts ripped from electrical switches, high-quality surgical equipment, sections of permanent magnets, measuring devices—tungsten from every possible source, gathered feverishly from all the settlements.

Dark mist lay spread over the tungsten mound. Occasionally, a night moth fluttered down, attracted by the glow of reflected starlight. The moth hung momentarily, beat its elongated wings futilely against the interwoven tangle of metal and then drifted off, into the shadows of the thick-packed vines that rose up from the stumps of sewer pipes.

'Not a very damn pretty spot,' Perine said wryly.

'Don't kid yourself,' O'Neill retorted. 'This is the prettiest spot on Earth. This is the spot that marks the grave of the autofac network. People are going to come around here looking for it someday. There's going to be a plaque here a mile high.'

'You're trying to keep your morale up,' Morrison snorted. 'You don't believe they're going to slaughter themselves over a heap of surgical tools and light-bulb filaments. They've probably got a machine down in the bottom level that sucks tungsten out of rock.'

'Maybe,' O'Neill said, slapping at a mosquito. The insect dodged cannily and then buzzed over to annoy Perine. Perine swung viciously at it and squatted sullenly down against the damp vegetation.

And there was what they had come to see.

O'Neill realized with a start that he had been looking at it for several minutes without recognizing it. The search-bug lay absolutely still. It rested at the crest of a small rise of slag, its anterior end slightly raised, receptors fully extended. It might have been an abandoned hulk; there was no activity of any kind, no sign of life or consciousness. The search-bug fitted perfectly into the wasted, fire-drenched landscape. A vague tub of metal sheets and gears and flat treads, it rested and waited. And watched.

It was examining the heap of tungsten. The bait had drawn its first bite.

'Fish,' Perine said thickly. 'The line moved. I think the sinker dropped.'

'What the hell are you mumbling about?' Morrison grunted. And then he, too, saw the search-bug. 'Jesus,' he whispered. He half rose to his feet, massive body arched forward. 'Well, there's *one* of them. Now all we need is a unit from the other factory. Which do you suppose it is?'

O'Neill located the communication vane and traced its angle. 'Pittsburgh, so pray for Detroit . . . pray like mad.'

Satisfied, the search-bug detached itself and rolled forward. Cautiously approaching the mound, it began a series of intricate maneuvers, rolling first one way and then another. The three watching men were mystified—until they glimpsed the first probing stalks of other search-bugs.

'Communication,' O'Neill said softly. 'Like bees.'

Now five Pittsburgh search-bugs were approaching the mound of tungsten products. Receptors waving excitedly, they increased their pace, scurrying in a sudden burst of discovery up the side of the mound to the top. A bug burrowed and rapidly disappeared. The whole mound shuddered; the bug was down inside, exploring the extent of the find.

Ten minutes later, the first Pittsburgh ore carts appeared and began industriously hurrying off with their haul.

'Damn it!' O'Neill said, agonized. 'They'll have it all before Detroit shows up.'

'Can't we do anything to slow them down?' Perine demanded helplessly. Leaping to his feet, he grabbed up a rock and heaved it at the nearest cart. The rock bounced off and the cart continued its work, unperturbed.

O'Neill got to his feet and prowled around, body rigid with impotent fury. Where were they? The autofacs were equal in all respects and the spot was the exact same linear distance from each center. Theoretically, the parties should have arrived simultaneously. Yet there was no sign of Detroit—and the final pieces of tungsten were being loaded before his eyes.

But then something streaked past him.

He didn't recognize it, for the object moved too quickly. It shot like a bullet among the tangled vines, raced up the side of the hill-crest, poised for an instant to aim itself and hurtled down the far side. It smashed directly into the lead cart. Projectile and victim shattered in an abrupt burst of sound.

Morrison leaped up. 'What the hell?'

'That's it!' Perine screamed, dancing around and waving his skinny arms. 'It's Detroit!'

A second Detroit search-bug appeared, hesitated as it took in the situation, and then flung itself furiously at the retreating Pittsburgh carts. Fragments of tungsten scattered everywhere—parts, wiring, broken plates, gears and springs and bolts of the two antagonists flew in all directions. The remaining carts wheeled screechingly; one of them dumped its load and rattled off at top speed. A second followed, still weighed down with tungsten. A Detroit search-bug caught up with it, spun directly in its path and neatly overturned it. Bug and cart rolled down a shallow trench, into a stagnant pool of water. Dripping and glistening, the two of them struggled, half submerged.

'Well,' O'Neill said unsteadily, 'we did it. We can start back home.' His legs felt weak. 'Where's our vehicle?'

As he gunned the truck motor, something flashed a long way off, something large and metallic, moving over the dead slag and ash. It was a dense clot of carts, a solid expanse of heavy-duty ore carriers racing to the scene. Which factory were they from?

It didn't matter, for out of the thick tangle of black dripping vines, a web of counter-extensions was creeping to meet them. Both factories were assembling their mobile units. From all directions, bugs slithered and crept, closing in around the remaining heap of tungsten. Neither factory was going to let needed raw material get away; neither was going to give up its find. Blindly, mechanically, in the grip of inflexible directives, the two opponents labored to assemble superior forces.

'Come on,' Morrison said urgently. 'Let's get out of here. All hell is bursting loose.'

O'Neill hastily turned the truck in the direction of the settlement. They began rumbling through the darkness on their way back. Every now and then, a metallic shape shot by them, going in the opposite direction.

'Did you see the load in that last cart?' Perine asked, worried. 'It wasn't empty.'

Neither were the carts that followed it, a whole procession of bulging supply carriers directed by an elaborate high-level surveying unit.

'Guns,' Morrison said, eyes wide with apprehension. 'They're taking in weapons. But who's going to use them?'

'They are,' O'Neill answered. He indicated a movement to their right. 'Look over there. This is something we hadn't expected.'

They were seeing the first factory representative move into action.

As the truck pulled into the Kansas City settlement, Judith hurried breathlessly toward them. Fluttering in her hand was a strip of metal-foil paper.

'What is it?' O'Neill demanded, grabbing it from her.

'Just come.' His wife struggled to catch her breath. 'A mobile car—raced up, dropped it off—and left. Big excitement. Golly, the factory's—a blaze of lights. You can see it for miles.'

O'Neill scanned the paper. It was a factory certification for the last group of settlement-placed orders, a total tabulation of requested and factory-analyzed needs. Stamped across the list in heavy black type were six foreboding words:

ALL SHIPMENTS SUSPENDED UNTIL FURTHER NOTICE

Letting out his breath harshly, O'Neill handed the paper over to Perine. 'No more consumer goods,' he said ironically, a nervous grin twitching across his face. 'The network's going on a wartime footing.'

'Then we did it?' Morrison asked haltingly.

'That's right,' O'Neill said. Now that the conflict had been sparked, he felt a growing, frigid terror. 'Pittsburgh and Detroit are in it to the finish. It's too late for us to change our minds, now—they're lining up allies.'

IV

Cool morning sunlight lay across the ruined plain of black metallic ash. The ash smoldered a dull, unhealthy red; it was still warm.

'Watch your step,' O'Neill cautioned. Grabbing hold of his wife's arm, he led her from the rusty, sagging truck, up onto the top of a pile of strewn concrete blocks, the scattered remains of a pillbox installation. Earl Perine followed, making his way carefully, hesitantly.

Behind them, the dilapidated settlement lay spread out, a disorderly checkerboard of houses, buildings and streets. Since the autofac network had closed down its supply and maintenance, the human settlements had fallen into semibarbarism. The commodities that remained were broken and only partly usable. It had been over a year since the last mobile factory truck had appeared, loaded with food, tools, clothing and repair parts. From the flat expanse of dark concrete and metal at the foot of the mountains, nothing had emerged in their direction.

Their wish had been granted—they were cut off, detached from the network.

On their own.

Around the settlement grew ragged fields of wheat and tattered stalks of sunbaked vegetables. Crude handmade tools had been distributed, primitive artifacts hammered out with great labor by the various settlements. The settlements were linked only by horsedrawn carts and by the slow stutter of the telegraph key.

They had managed to keep their organization, though. Goods and services were exchanged on a slow, steady basis. Basic commodities were produced and distributed. The clothing that O'Neill and his wife and Earl Perine wore was coarse and unbleached, but sturdy. And they had managed to convert a few of the trucks from gasoline to wood.

'Here we are,' O'Neill said. 'We can see from here.'

'Is it worth it?' Judith asked, exhausted. Bending down, she plucked aimlessly at her shoe, trying to dig a pebble from the soft hide sole. 'It's a long way to come, to see something we've seen every day for thirteen months.'

'True,' O'Neill admitted, his hand briefly resting on his wife's limp shoulder. 'But this may be the last. And that's what we want to see.'

In the gray sky above them, a swift circling dot of opaque black moved. High, remote, the dot spun and darted, following an intricate and wary course. Gradually, its gyrations moved it toward the mountains and the bleak expanse of bomb-rubbled structure sunk in their base.

'San Francisco,' O'Neill explained. 'One of those long-range hawk projectiles, all the way from the West Coast.'

'And you think it's the last?' Perine asked.

'It's the only one we've seen this month.' O'Neill seated himself and began sprinkling dried bits of tobacco into a trench of brown paper. 'And we used to see hundreds.'

'Maybe they have something better,' Judith suggested. She found a smooth rock and tiredly seated herself. 'Could it be?'

Her husband smiled ironically. 'No. They don't have anything better.'

The three of them were tensely silent. Above them, the circling dot of black drew closer. There was no sign of activity from the flat surface of metal and concrete; the Kansas City factory remained inert, totally unresponsive. A few billows of warm ash drifted across it and one end was partly submerged in rubble. The factory had taken numerous direct hits. Across the plain, the furrows of its subsurface tunnels lay exposed, clogged with debris and the dark, water-seeking tendrils of tough vines.

'Those damn vines,' Perine grumbled, picking at an old sore on his unshaven chin. 'They're taking over the world.'

Here and there around the factory, the demolished ruin of a mobile extension rusted in the morning dew. Carts, trucks, search-bugs, factory representatives, weapons carriers, guns, supply trains, subsurface projectiles, indiscriminate parts of machinery mixed and fused together in shapeless piles. Some had been destroyed returning to the factory; others had been contacted as they emerged, fully loaded, heavy with equipment. The factory itself—what remained of it—seemed to have settled more deeply into the earth. Its upper surface was barely visible, almost lost in drifting ash.

In four days, there had been no known activity, no visible movement of any sort.

'It's dead,' Perine said. 'You can see it's dead.'

O'Neill didn't answer. Squatting down, he made himself comfortable and prepared to wait. In his own mind, he was sure that some fragment of automation remained in the eroded factory. Time would tell. He examined his wristwatch; it was eight thirty. In the old days, the factory would be starting its daily routine. Processions of trucks and varied mobile units would be coming to the surface, loaded with supplies, to begin their expeditions to the human settlement.

Off to the right, something stirred. He quickly turned his attention to it.

A single battered ore-gathering cart was creeping clumsily toward the factory. One last damaged mobile unit trying to complete its task. The cart was virtually empty; a few meager scraps of metal lay strewn in its hold. A scavenger . . . the metal was sections ripped from destroyed equipment encountered on the way. Feebly, like a blind metallic insect, the cart approached the factory. Its progress was incredibly jerky. Every now and then, it halted, bucked and quivered, and wandered aimlessly off the path.

'Control is bad,' Judith said, with a touch of horror in her voice. 'The factory's having trouble guiding it back.'

Yes, he had seen that. Around New York, the factory had lost its high-frequency transmitter completely. Its mobile units had floundered in crazy gyrations, racing in random circles, crashing against rocks and trees, sliding into gullies, overturning, finally unwinding and becoming reluctantly inanimate.

The ore cart reached the edge of the ruined plain and halted briefly. Above it, the dot of black still circled the sky. For a time, the cart remained frozen.

'The factory's trying to decide,' Perine said. 'It needs the material, but it's afraid of that hawk up there.'

The factory debated and nothing stirred. Then the ore cart again resumed its unsteady crawl. It left the tangle of vines and started out across the blasted open plain. Painfully, with infinite caution, it headed toward the slab of dark concrete and metal at the base of the mountains.

The hawk stopped circling.

'Get down!' O'Neill said sharply. 'They've got those rigged with the new bombs.'

His wife and Perine crouched down beside him and the three of them peered warily at the plain and the metal insect crawling laboriously across it. In the sky, the hawk swept in a straight line until it hung directly over the cart. Then, without a sound or warning, it came down in a straight dive. Hands to her face, Judith shrieked, 'I can't watch! It's awful! Like wild animals!'

'It's not after the cart,' O'Neill grated.

As the airborne projectile dropped, the cart put on a burst of desperate speed. It raced noisily toward the factory, clanking and rattling, trying in a last futile attempt to reach safety. Forgetting the menace above, the frantically eager factory opened up and guided its mobile unit directly inside. And the hawk had what it wanted.

Before the barrier could close, the hawk swooped down in a long glide parallel with the ground. As the cart disappeared into the depths of the factory, the hawk shot after it, a swift shimmer of metal that hurtled past the clanking cart. Suddenly aware, the factory snapped the barrier shut. Grotesquely, the cart struggled; it was caught fast in the half-closed entrance.

But whether it freed itself didn't matter. There was a dull rumbling stir. The ground moved, billowed, then settled back. A deep shock wave passed beneath the three watching human beings. From the factory rose a single column of black smoke. The surface of concrete split like a dried pod; it shriveled and broke, and dribbled shattered bits of itself in a shower of ruin. The smoke hung for a while, drifting aimlessly away with the morning wind.

The factory was a fused, gutted wreck. It had been penetrated and destroyed.

O'Neill got stiffly to his feet. 'That's all. All over with. We've got what we set out after—we've destroyed the autofac network.' He glanced at Perine. 'Or was that what we were after?'

They looked toward the settlement that lay behind them. Little remained of the orderly rows of houses and streets of the previous years. Without the network, the settlement had rapidly decayed. The original prosperous neatness had dissipated; the settlement was shabby, ill-kept.

'Of course,' Perine said haltingly. 'Once we get into the factories and start setting up our own assembly lines . . .'

'Is there anything left?' Judith inquired.

'There must be something left. My God, there were levels going down miles!'

'Some of those bombs they developed toward the end were awfully big,' Judith pointed out. 'Better than anything we had in our war.'

'Remember that camp we saw? The ruins-squatters?'

'I wasn't along,' Perine said.

'They were like wild animals. Eating roots and larvae. Sharpening rocks, tanning hides. Savagery, bestiality.'

'But that's what people like that want,' Perine answered defensively

'Do they? Do we want this?' O'Neill indicated the straggling settlement. 'Is this what we set out looking for, that day we collected the tungsten? Or that day we told the factory truck its milk was—' He couldn't remember the word.

'Pizzled,' Judith supplied.

'Come on,' O'Neill said. 'Let's get started. Let's see what's left of that factory—left for us.'

★

They approached the ruined factory late in the afternoon. Four trucks rumbled shakily up to the rim of the gutted pit and halted, motors steaming, tailpipes dripping. Wary and alert, workmen scrambled down and stepped gingerly across the hot ash.

'Maybe it's too soon,' one of them objected.

O'Neill had no intention of waiting. 'Come on,' he ordered. Grabbing up a flashlight, he stepped down into the crater.

The sheltered hull of the Kansas City factory lay directly ahead. In its gutted mouth, the ore cart still hung caught, but it was no longer struggling. Beyond the cart was an ominous pool of gloom. O'Neill flashed his light through the entrance; the tangled, jagged remains of upright supports were visible.

'We want to get down deep,' he said to Morrison, who prowled cautiously beside him. 'If there's anything left, it's at the bottom.'

Morrison grunted. 'Those boring moles from Atlanta got most of the deep layers.'

'Until the others got their mines sunk.' O'Neill stepped carefully through the sagging entrance, climbed a heap of debris that had been tossed against the slit from inside, and found himself within the factory—an expanse of confused wreckage, without pattern or meaning.

'Entropy,' Morrison breathed, oppressed. 'The thing it always hated. The thing it was built to fight. Random particles everywhere. No purpose to it.'

'Down underneath,' O'Neill said stubbornly, 'we may find some sealed enclaves. I know they got so they were dividing up into autonomous sections, trying to preserve repair units intact, to re-form the composite factory.'

'The moles got most of them, too,' Morrison observed, but he lumbered after O'Neill.

Behind them, the workmen came slowly. A section of wreckage shifted ominously and a shower of hot fragments cascaded down.

'You men get back to the trucks,' O'Neill said. 'No sense endangering any more of us than we have to. If Morrison and I don't come back, forget us—don't risk sending a rescue party.' As they left, he pointed out to Morrison a descending ramp still partially intact. 'Let's get below.'

Silently, the two men passed one dead level after another. Endless miles of dark ruin stretched out, without sound or activity. The vague shapes of darkened machinery, unmoving belts and conveyer equipment were partially visible, and the partially completed husks of war projectiles, bent and twisted by the final blast.

'We can salvage some of that,' O'Neill said, but he didn't actually believe it. The machinery was fused, shapeless. Everything in the factory had run together, molten slag without form or use. 'Once we get it to the surface . . .'

'We can't,' Morrison contradicted bitterly. 'We don't have hoists or winches.' He kicked at a heap of charred supplies that had stopped along its broken belt and spilled halfway across the ramp.

'It seemed like a good idea at the time,' O'Neill said as the two of them continued past vacant levels of machines. 'But now that I look back, I'm not so sure.'

They had penetrated a long way into the factory. The final level lay spread out ahead of them. O'Neill flashed the light here and there, trying to locate undestroyed sections, portions of the assembly process still intact.

It was Morrison who felt it first. He suddenly dropped to his hands and knees; heavy body pressed against the floor, he lay listening, face hard, eyes wide. 'For God's sake—'

'What is it?' O'Neill cried. Then he, too, felt it. Beneath

them, a faint, insistent vibration hummed through the floor, a steady hum of activity. They had been wrong; the hawk had not been totally successful. Below, in a deeper level, the factory was still alive. Closed, limited operations still went on.

'On its own,' O'Neill muttered, searching for an extension of the descent lift. 'Autonomous activity, set to continue after the rest is gone. How do we get down?'

The descent lift was broken off, sealed by a thick section of metal. The still-living layer beneath their feet was completely cut off; there was no entrance.

Racing back the way they had come, O'Neill reached the surface and hailed the first truck. 'Where the hell's the torch? Give it here!'

The precious blowtorch was passed to him and he hurried back, puffing, into the depths of the ruined factory where Morrison waited. Together, the two of them began frantically cutting through the warped metal flooring, burning apart the sealed layers of protective mesh.

'It's coming,' Morrison gasped, squinting in the glare of the torch. The plate fell with a clang, disappearing into the level below. A blaze of white light burst up around them and the two men leaped back.

In the sealed chamber, furious activity boomed and echoed, a steady process of moving belts, whirring machine-tools, fast-moving mechanical supervisors. At one end, a steady flow of raw materials entered the line; at the far end, the final product was whipped off, inspected and crammed into a conveyer tube.

All this was visible for a split second; then the intrusion was discovered. Robot relays came into play. The blaze of lights flickered and dimmed. The assembly line froze to a halt, stopped in its furious activity.

The machines clicked off and became silent.

At one end, a mobile unit detached itself and sped up the wall toward the hole O'Neill and Morrison had cut. It slammed an emergency seal in place and expertly welded it tight. The scene below was gone. A moment later the floor shivered as activity resumed.

Morrison, white-faced and shaking, turned to O'Neill. 'What are they doing? What are they making?'

'Not weapons,' O'Neill said.

'That stuff is being sent up'—Morrison gestured convulsively—'to the surface.'

Shakily, O'Neill climbed to his feet. 'Can we locate the spot?'

'I—think so'

'We better.' O'Neill swept up the flashlight and started toward the ascent ramp. 'We're going to have to see what those pellets are that they're shooting up.'

The exit valve of the conveyor tube was concealed in a tangle of vines and ruins a quarter of a mile beyond the factory. In a slot of rock at the base of the mountains the valve poked up like a nozzle. From ten yards away, it was invisible; the two men were almost on top of it before they noticed it.

Every few moments, a pellet burst from the valve and shot up into the sky. The nozzle revolved and altered its angle of deflection; each pellet was launched in a slightly varied trajectory.

'How far are they going?' Morrison wondered.

'Probably varies. It's distributing them at random.' O'Neill advanced cautiously, but the mechanism took no note of him. Plastered against the towering wall of rock was a crumpled pellet; by accident, the nozzle had released it directly at the mountainside. O'Neill climbed up, got it and jumped down.

The pellet was a smashed container of machinery, tiny metallic elements too minute to be analyzed without a microscope.

'Not a weapon,' O'Neill said.

The cylinder had split. At first he couldn't tell if it had been the impact or deliberate internal mechanisms at work. From the rent, an ooze of metal bits was sliding. Squatting down, O'Neill examined them.

The bits were in motion. Microscopic machinery, smaller than ants, smaller than pins, working energetically, purpose-fully—constructing something that looked like a tiny rectangle of steel.

'They're building,' O'Neill said, awed. He got up and prowled on. Off to the side, at the far edge of the gully, he came across a downed pellet far advanced on its construction. Apparently it had been released some time ago.

This one had made great enough progress to be identified. Minute as it was, the structure was familiar. The machinery was building a miniature replica of the demolished factory.

'Well,' O'Neill said thoughtfully, 'we're back where we started from. For better or worse . . . I don't know.'

'I guess they must be all over Earth by now,' Morrison said, 'landing everywhere and going to work.'

A thought struck O'Neill. 'Maybe some of them are geared to escape velocity. That would be neat—autofac networks throughout the whole universe.'

Behind him, the nozzle continued to spurt out its torrent of metal seeds.